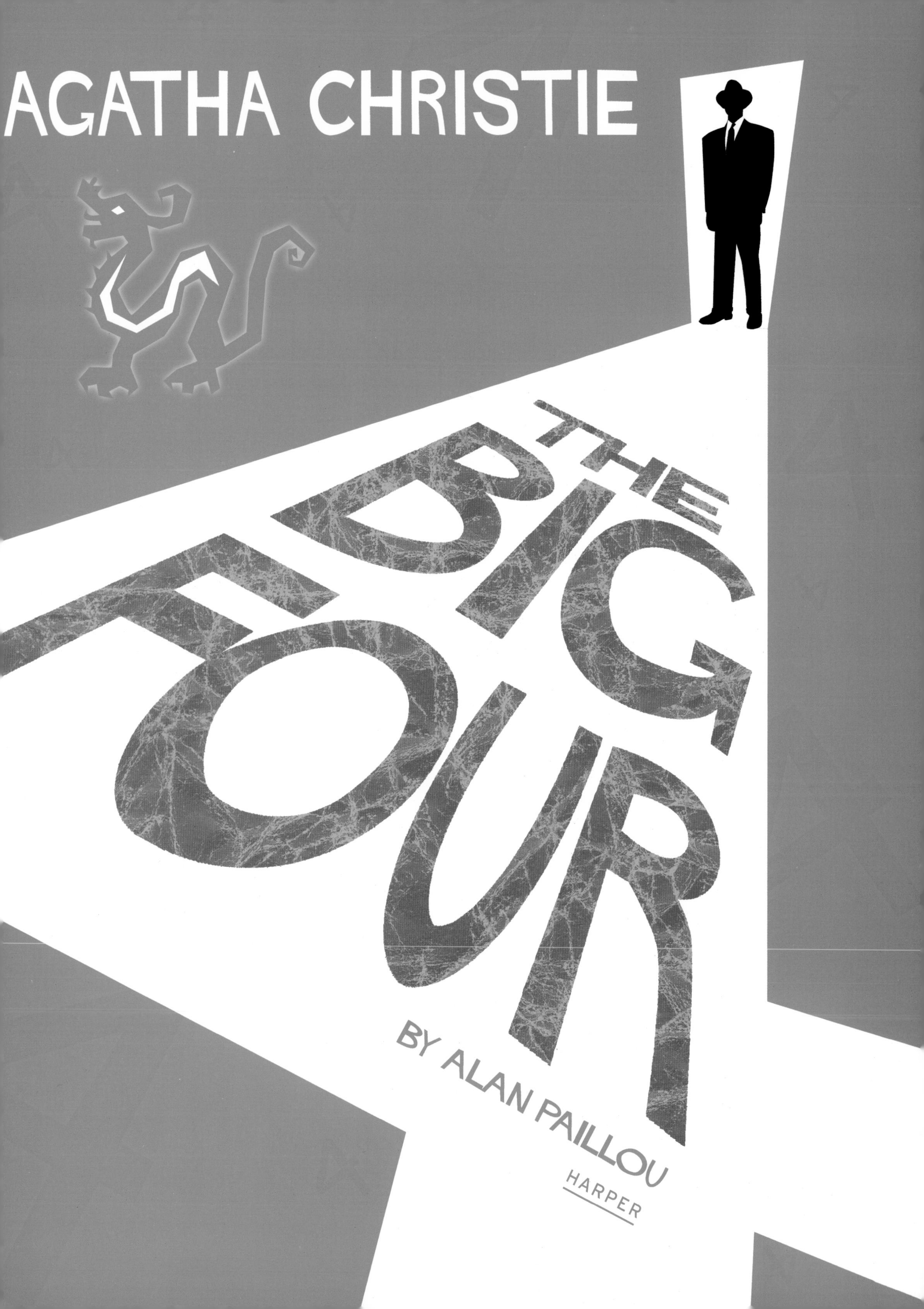
AGATHA CHRISTIE
THE BIG FOUR
BY ALAN PAILLOU
HARPER

A big thank you to Catherine and Jean-Blaise for their help.
— Alain Paillou

HARPER
An imprint of HarperCollins*Publishers*
77-85 Fulham Palace Road
Hammersmith, London W6 8JB
www.harpercollins.co.uk

First published by HARPER 2007
1

Comic book edition published in France as *Les Quatre*
© EP Editions 2006
Based on *The Big Four* © 1927 by Agatha Christie Limited,
a Chorion Company. All rights reserved.
www.agathachristie.com

Adapted and illustrated by Alain Paillou. Colour by Wilmaury.
English edition edited by David Brawn.

ISBN-13 978-0-00-725065-3
ISBN-10 0-00-725065-7

Printed and bound in Singapore by Imago

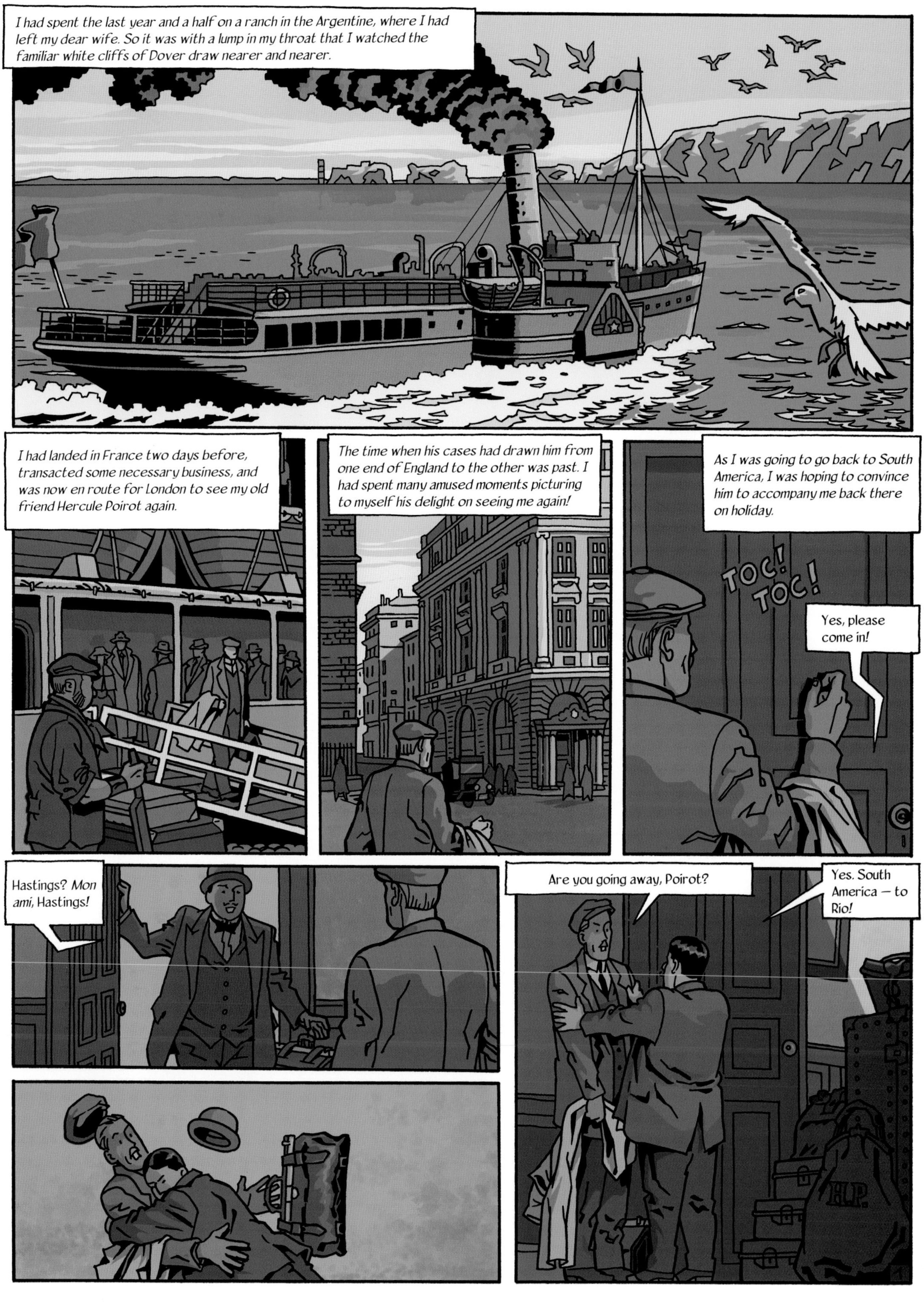
I had spent the last year and a half on a ranch in the Argentine, where I had left my dear wife. So it was with a lump in my throat that I watched the familiar white cliffs of Dover draw nearer and nearer.
I had landed in France two days before, transacted some necessary business, and was now en route for London to see my old friend Hercule Poirot again.
The time when his cases had drawn him from one end of England to the other was past. I had spent many amused moments picturing to myself his delight on seeing me again!
As I was going to go back to South America, I was hoping to convince him to accompany me back there on holiday.
TOC! TOC!
Yes, please come in!
Hastings? *Mon ami*, Hastings!
Are you going away, Poirot?
Yes. South America — to Rio!
H.P.

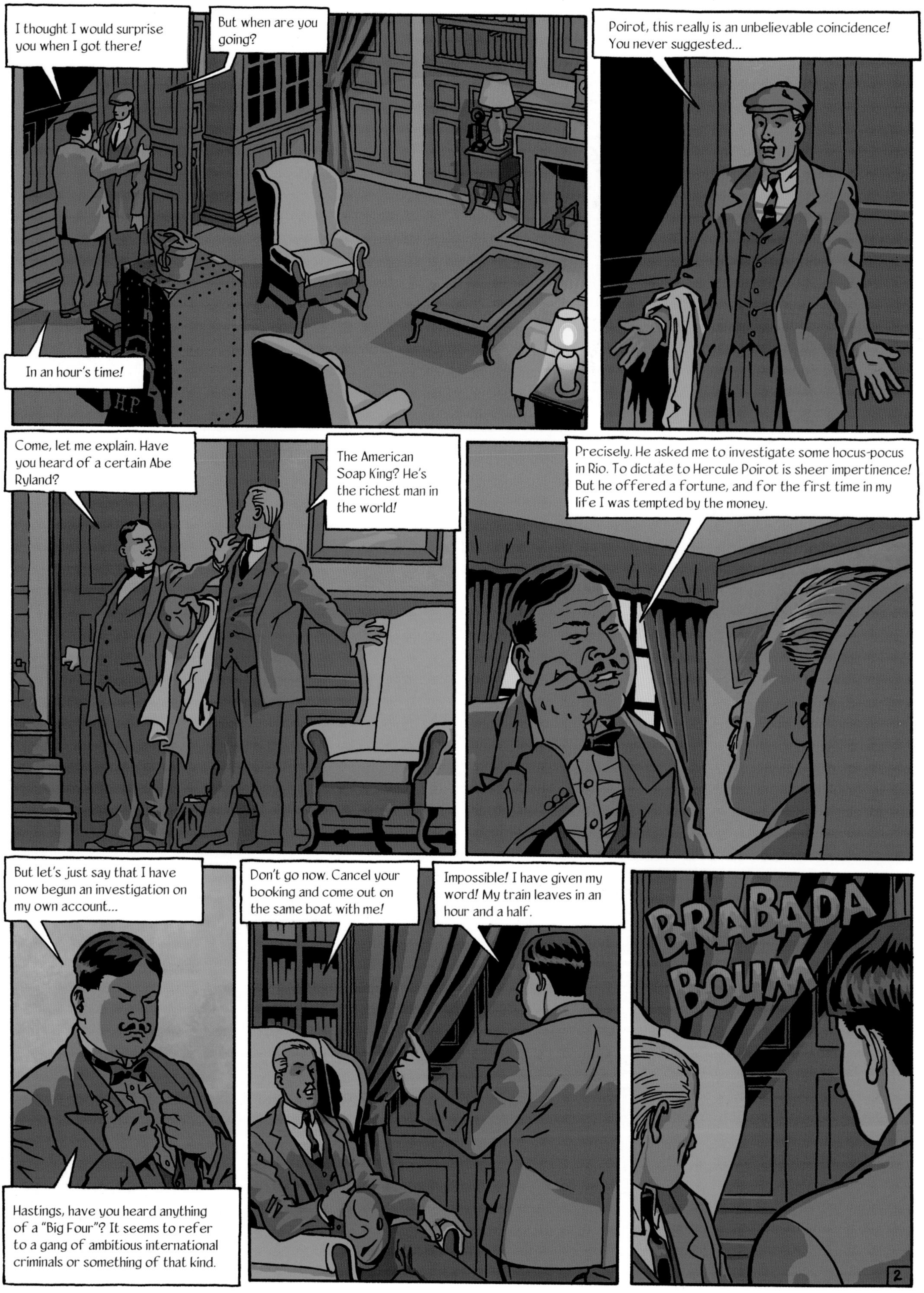
I thought I would surprise you when I got there!
But when are you going?
In an hour's time!
H.P.
Poirot, this really is an unbelievable coincidence! You never suggested...
Come, let me explain. Have you heard of a certain Abe Ryland?
The American Soap King? He's the richest man in the world!
Precisely. He asked me to investigate some hocus-pocus in Rio. To dictate to Hercule Poirot is sheer impertinence! But he offered a fortune, and for the first time in my life I was tempted by the money.
But let's just say that I have now begun an investigation on my own account...
Hastings, have you heard anything of a "Big Four"? It seems to refer to a gang of ambitious international criminals or something of that kind.
Don't go now. Cancel your booking and come out on the same boat with me!
Impossible! I have given my word! My train leaves in an hour and a half.
BRABADA BOUM
2

Hercule Poirot, 14 Farraway Street?!

Hercule Poirot... 14 Farraway Street...

The Big Four... Li Chang Yen, the brains of the Big Four... He is Number One!

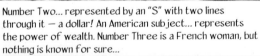

Number Two... represented by an "S" with two lines through it — a dollar! An American subject... represents the power of wealth. Number Three is a French woman, but nothing is known for sure...

Number Four is... the *Destroyer!*

Mon Dieu! I was right then...!

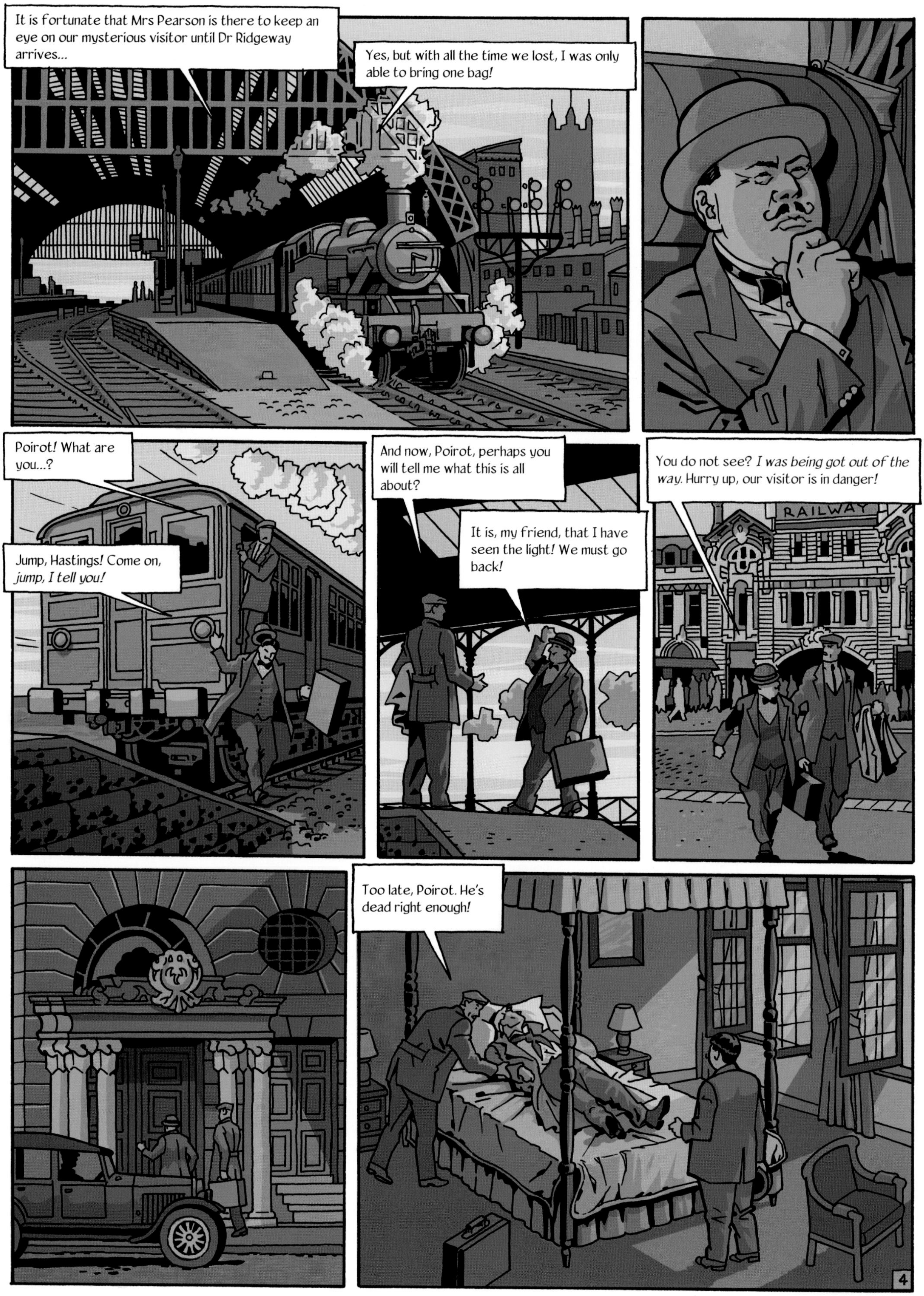

It is fortunate that Mrs Pearson is there to keep an eye on our mysterious visitor until Dr Ridgeway arrives...
Yes, but with all the time we lost, I was only able to bring one bag!
Poirot! What are you...?
Jump, Hastings! Come on, *jump, I tell you!*
And now, Poirot, perhaps you will tell me what this is all about?
It is, my friend, that I have seen the light! We must go back!
You do not see? *I was being got out of the way*. Hurry up, our visitor is in danger!
RAILWAY
Too late, Poirot. He's dead right enough!
4

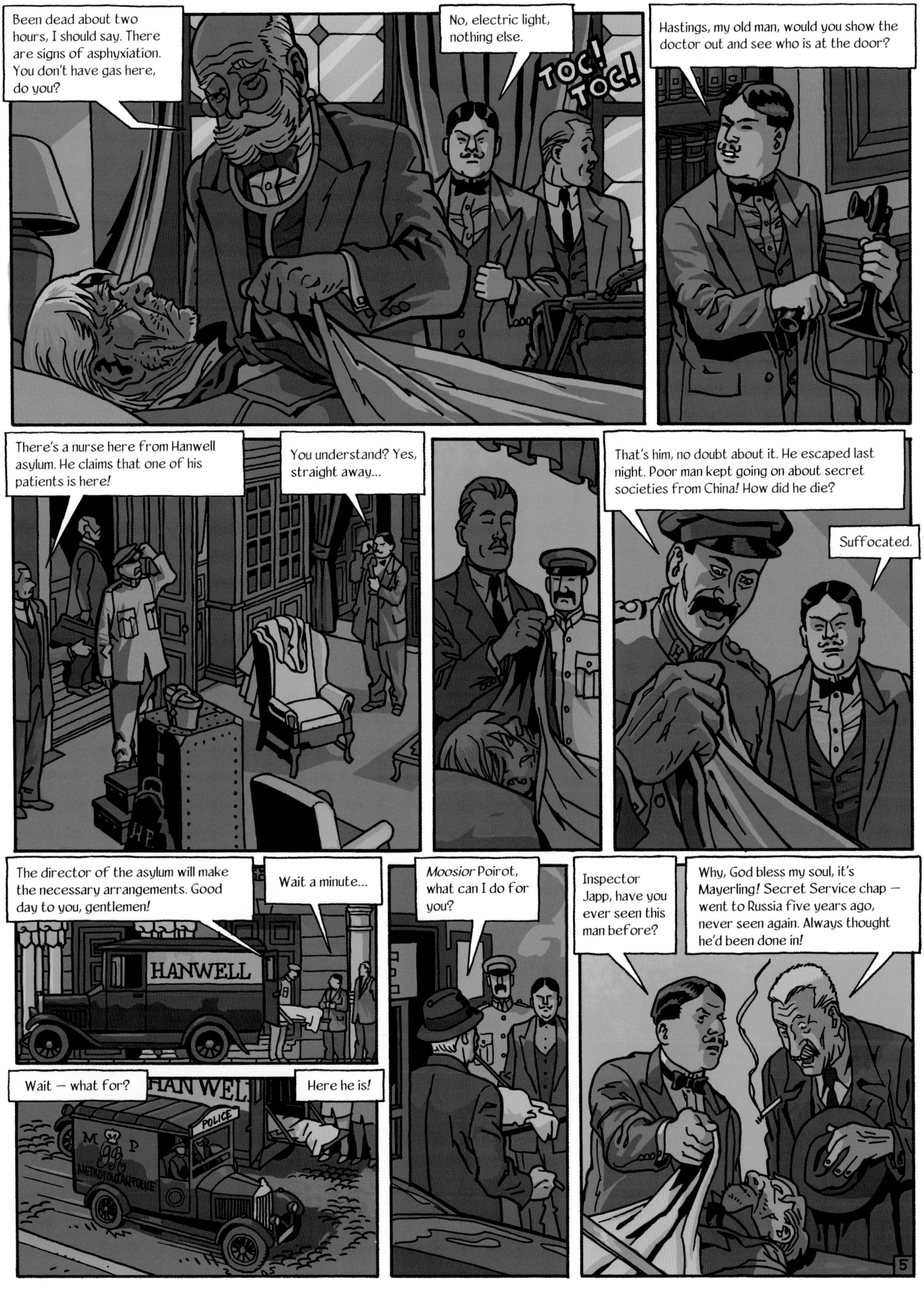

Been dead about two hours, I should say. There are signs of asphyxiation. You don't have gas here, do you?
No, electric light, nothing else.
TOC! TOC!
Hastings, my old man, would you show the doctor out and see who is at the door?
There's a nurse here from Hanwell asylum. He claims that one of his patients is here!
You understand? Yes, straight away...
That's him, no doubt about it. He escaped last night. Poor man kept going on about secret societies from China! How did he die?
Suffocated.
The director of the asylum will make the necessary arrangements. Good day to you, gentlemen!
Wait a minute...
HANWELL
Wait – what for?
Here he is!
POLICE
METROPOLITAN POLICE
Moosior Poirot, what can I do for you?
Inspector Japp, have you ever seen this man before?
Why, God bless my soul, it's Mayerling! Secret Service chap – went to Russia five years ago, never seen again. Always thought he'd been done in!
5

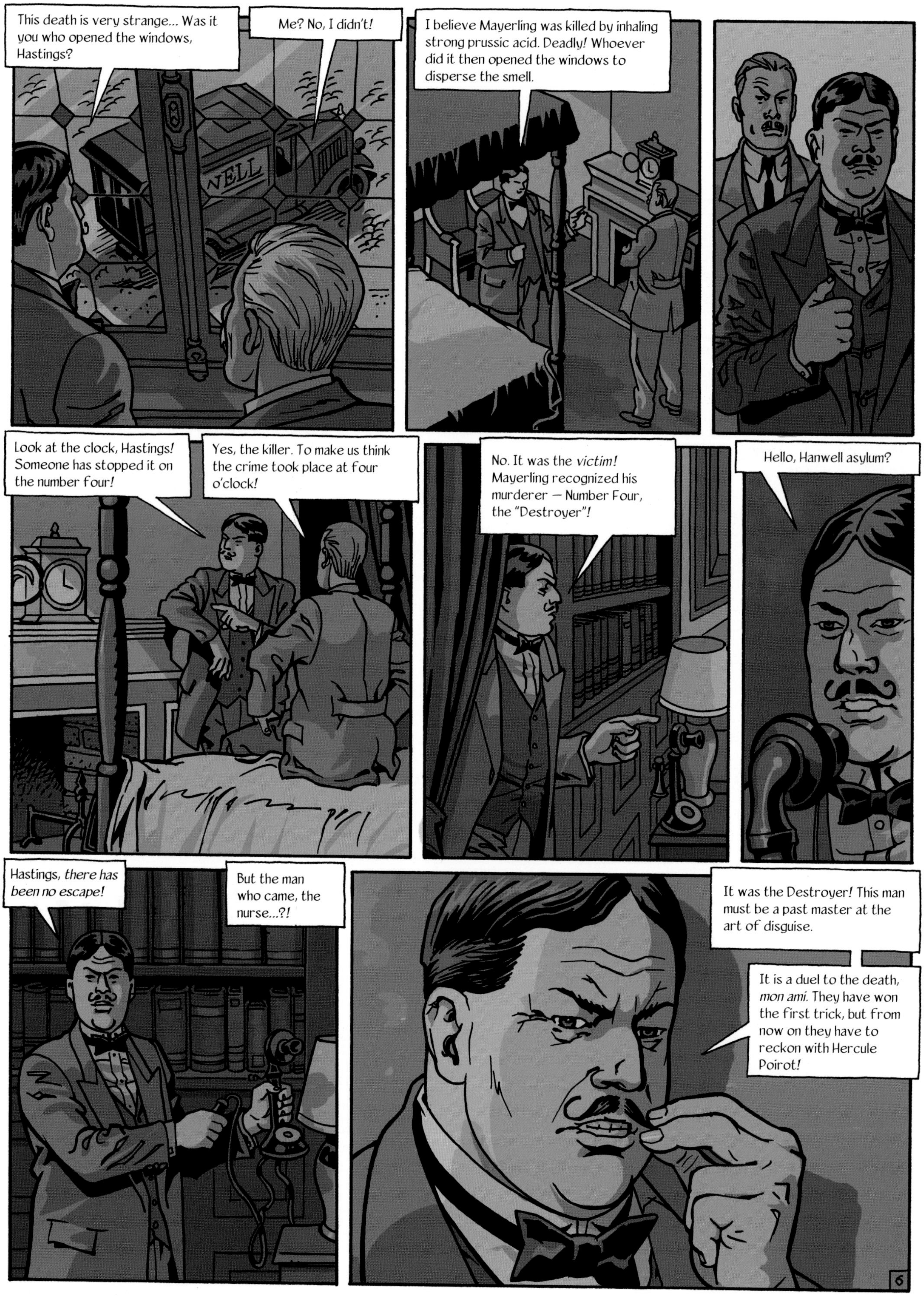
This death is very strange... Was it you who opened the windows, Hastings?
Me? No, I didn't!
I believe Mayerling was killed by inhaling strong prussic acid. Deadly! Whoever did it then opened the windows to disperse the smell.
Look at the clock, Hastings! Someone has stopped it on the number four!
Yes, the killer. To make us think the crime took place at four o'clock!
No. It was the *victim!* Mayerling recognized his murderer — Number Four, the "Destroyer"!
Hello, Hanwell asylum?
Hastings, *there has been no escape!*
But the man who came, the nurse...?!
It was the Destroyer! This man must be a past master at the art of disguise.
It is a duel to the death, *mon ami.* They have won the first trick, but from now on they have to reckon with Hercule Poirot!
6

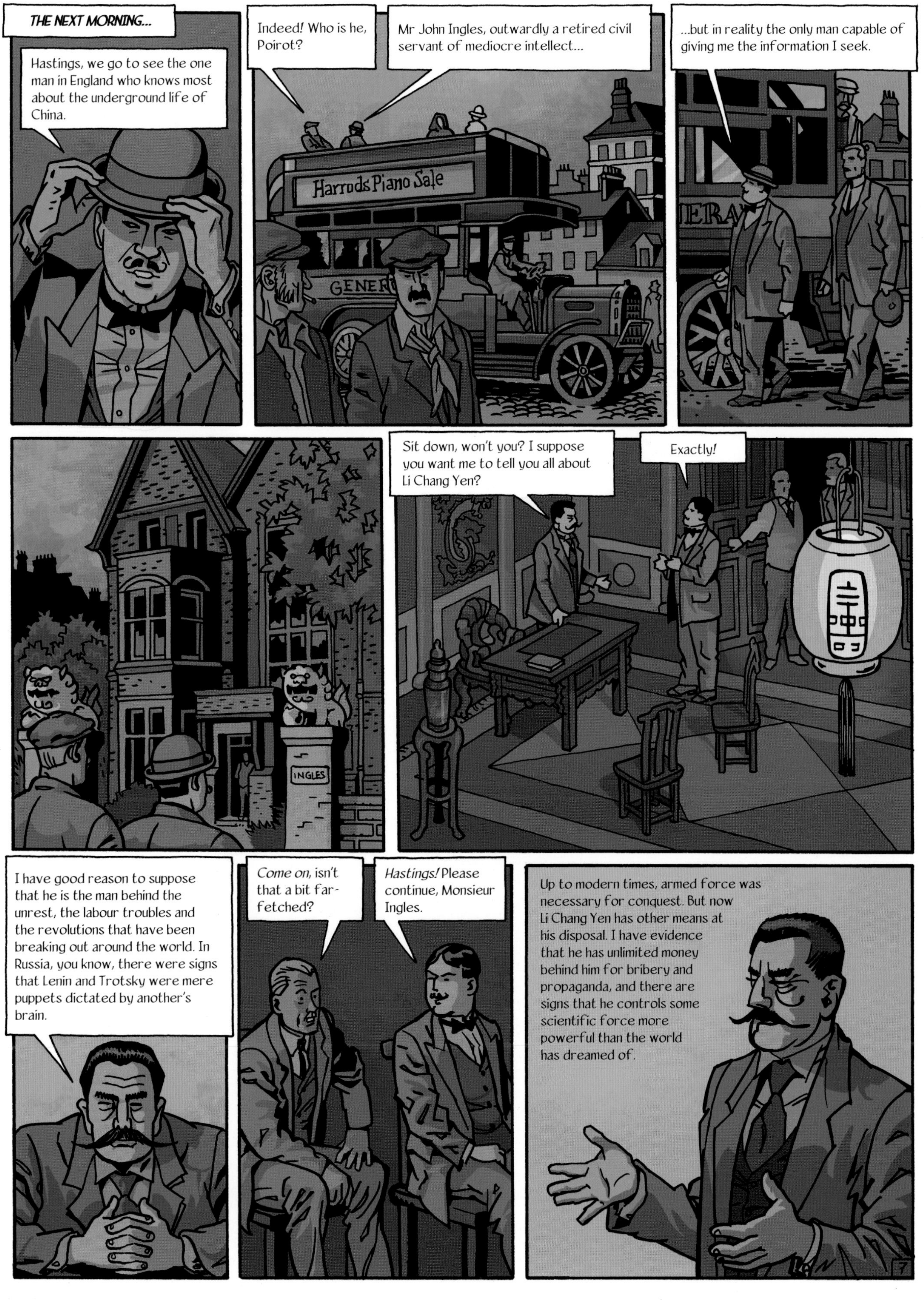

THE NEXT MORNING...
Hastings, we go to see the one man in England who knows most about the underground life of China.
Indeed! Who is he, Poirot?
Mr John Ingles, outwardly a retired civil servant of mediocre intellect...
Harrods Piano Sale
GENER
...but in reality the only man capable of giving me the information I seek.
INGLES
Sit down, won't you? I suppose you want me to tell you all about Li Chang Yen?
Exactly!
I have good reason to suppose that he is the man behind the unrest, the labour troubles and the revolutions that have been breaking out around the world. In Russia, you know, there were signs that Lenin and Trotsky were mere puppets dictated by another's brain.
Come on, isn't that a bit far-fetched?
Hastings! Please continue, Monsieur Ingles.
Up to modern times, armed force was necessary for conquest. But now Li Chang Yen has other means at his disposal. I have evidence that he has unlimited money behind him for bribery and propaganda, and there are signs that he controls some scientific force more powerful than the world has dreamed of.
7

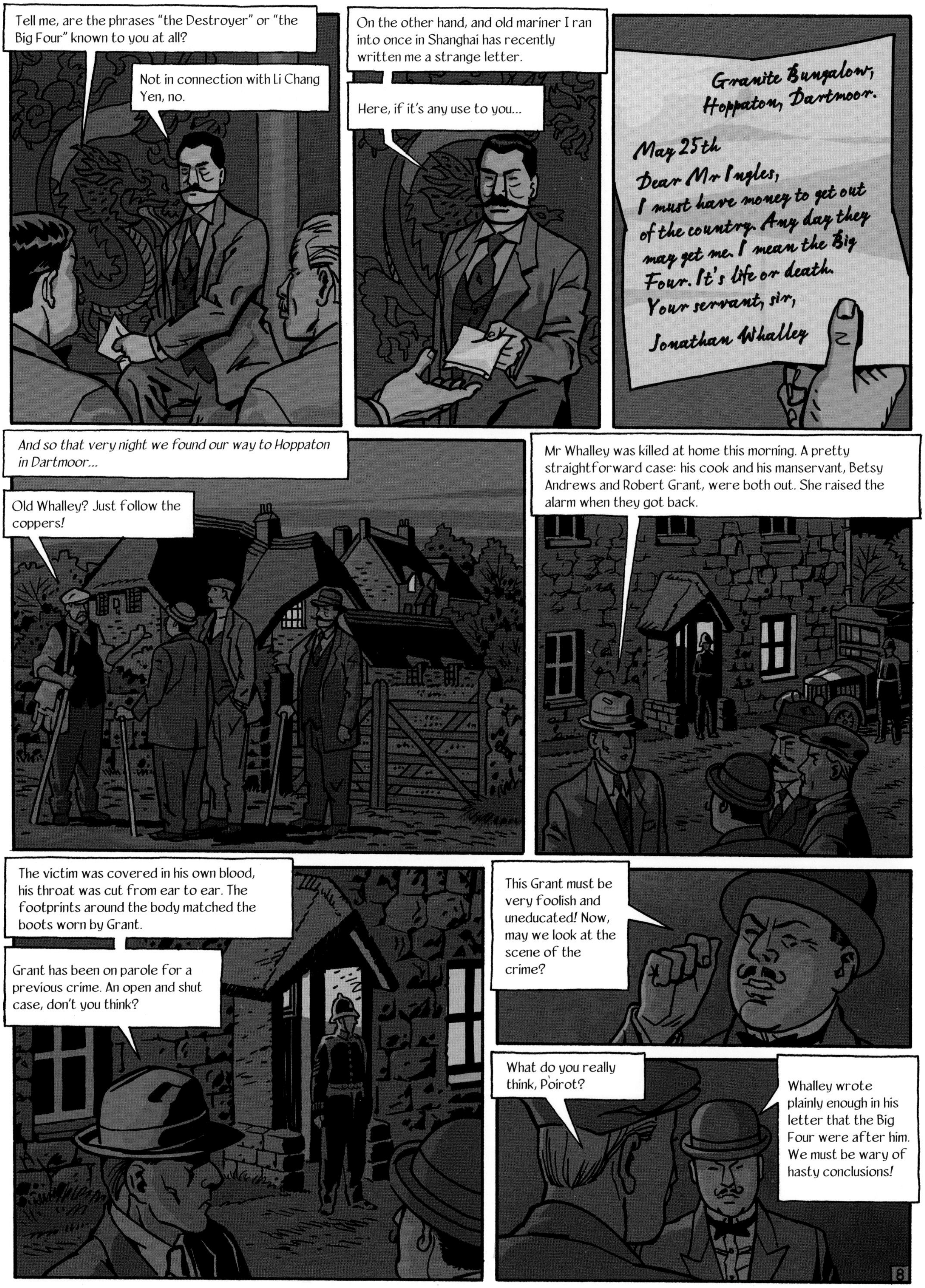

Tell me, are the phrases "the Destroyer" or "the Big Four" known to you at all?
Not in connection with Li Chang Yen, no.
On the other hand, and old mariner I ran into once in Shanghai has recently written me a strange letter.
Here, if it's any use to you...
Granite Bungalow, Hoppaton, Dartmoor.
May 25th
Dear Mr Ingles,
I must have money to get out of the country. Any day they may get me. I mean the Big Four. It's life or death.
Your servant, sir,
Jonathan Whalley
And so that very night we found our way to Hoppaton in Dartmoor...
Old Whalley? Just follow the coppers!
Mr Whalley was killed at home this morning. A pretty straightforward case: his cook and his manservant, Betsy Andrews and Robert Grant, were both out. She raised the alarm when they got back.
The victim was covered in his own blood, his throat was cut from ear to ear. The footprints around the body matched the boots worn by Grant.
Grant has been on parole for a previous crime. An open and shut case, don't you think?
This Grant must be very foolish and uneducated! Now, may we look at the scene of the crime?
What do you really think, Poirot?
Whalley wrote plainly enough in his letter that the Big Four were after him. We must be wary of hasty conclusions!
8

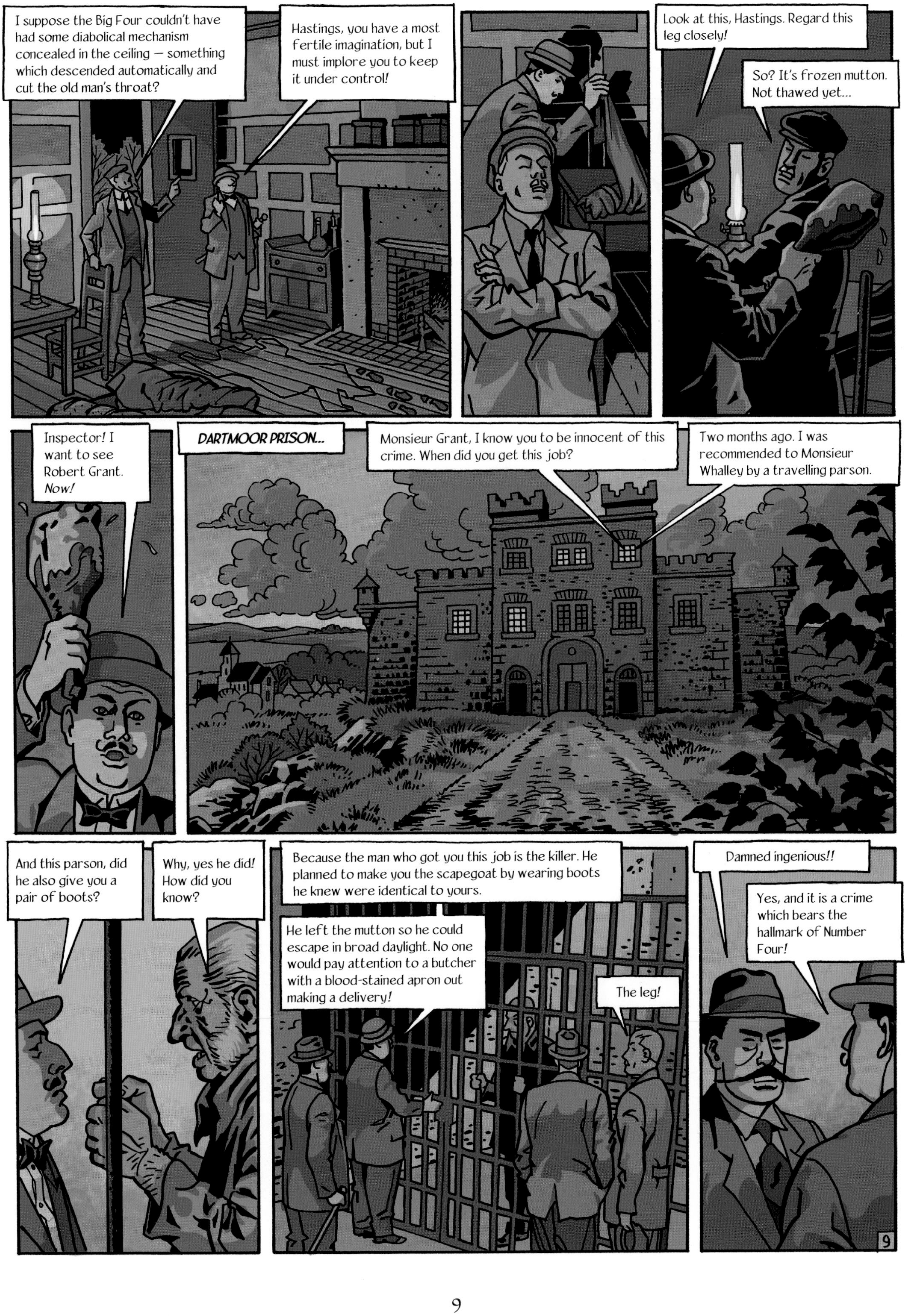
I suppose the Big Four couldn't have had some diabolical mechanism concealed in the ceiling — something which descended automatically and cut the old man's throat?
Hastings, you have a most fertile imagination, but I must implore you to keep it under control!
Look at this, Hastings. Regard this leg closely!
So? It's frozen mutton. Not thawed yet...
Inspector! I want to see Robert Grant. Now!
DARTMOOR PRISON...
Monsieur Grant, I know you to be innocent of this crime. When did you get this job?
Two months ago. I was recommended to Monsieur Whalley by a travelling parson.
And this parson, did he also give you a pair of boots?
Why, yes he did! How did you know?
Because the man who got you this job is the killer. He planned to make you the scapegoat by wearing boots he knew were identical to yours.
He left the mutton so he could escape in broad daylight. No one would pay attention to a butcher with a blood-stained apron out making a delivery!
The leg!
Damned ingenious!!
Yes, and it is a crime which bears the hallmark of Number Four!
9

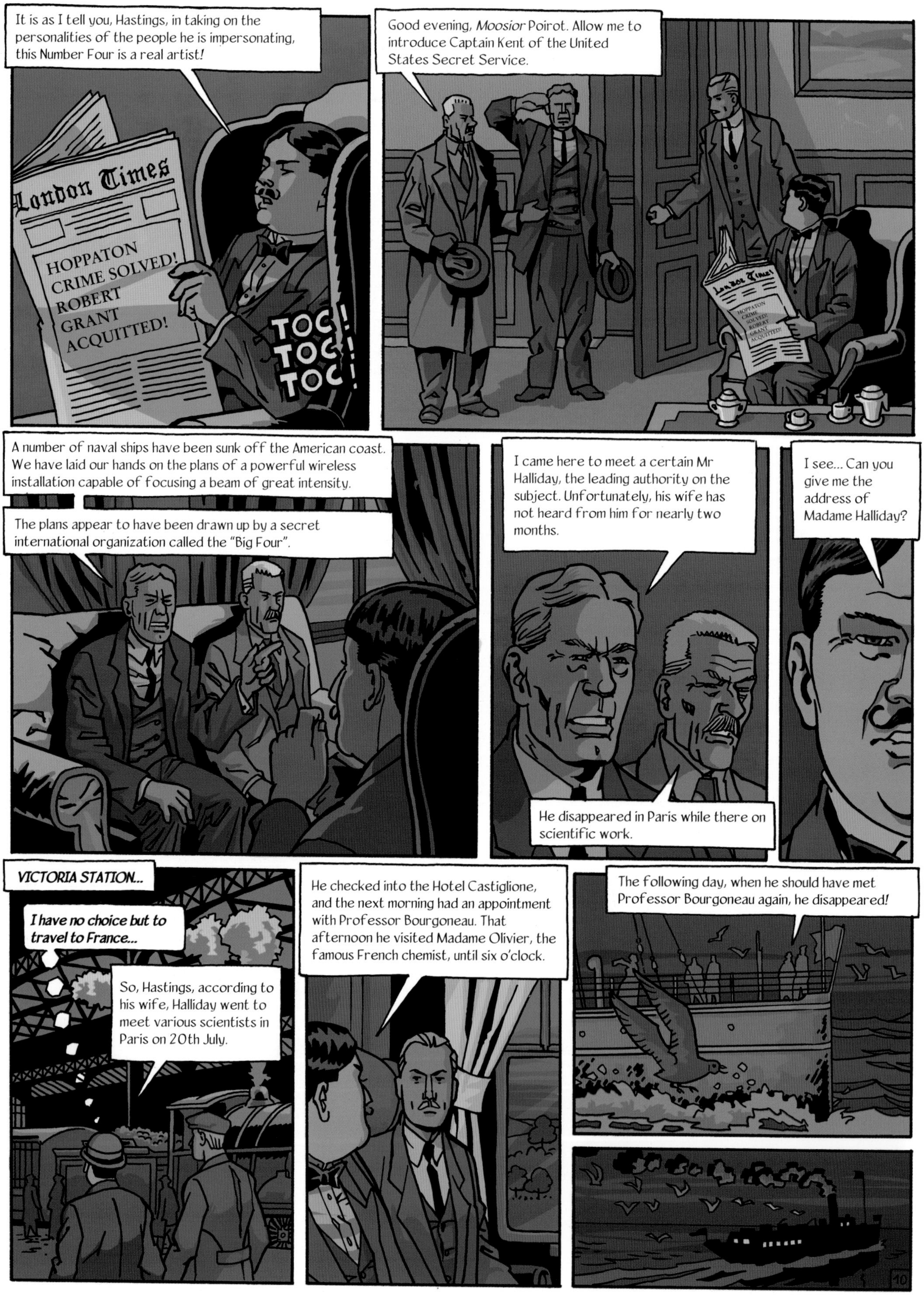
It is as I tell you, Hastings, in taking on the personalities of the people he is impersonating, this Number Four is a real artist!
London Times
HOPPATON CRIME SOLVED! ROBERT GRANT ACQUITTED!
TOC! TOC! TOC!
Good evening, *Moosior* Poirot. Allow me to introduce Captain Kent of the United States Secret Service.
A number of naval ships have been sunk off the American coast. We have laid our hands on the plans of a powerful wireless installation capable of focusing a beam of great intensity.
The plans appear to have been drawn up by a secret international organization called the "Big Four".
I came here to meet a certain Mr Halliday, the leading authority on the subject. Unfortunately, his wife has not heard from him for nearly two months.
He disappeared in Paris while there on scientific work.
I see... Can you give me the address of Madame Halliday?
VICTORIA STATION...
I have no choice but to travel to France...
So, Hastings, according to his wife, Halliday went to meet various scientists in Paris on 20th July.
He checked into the Hotel Castiglione, and the next morning had an appointment with Professor Bourgoneau. That afternoon he visited Madame Olivier, the famous French chemist, until six o'clock.
The following day, when he should have met Professor Bourgoneau again, he disappeared!
10

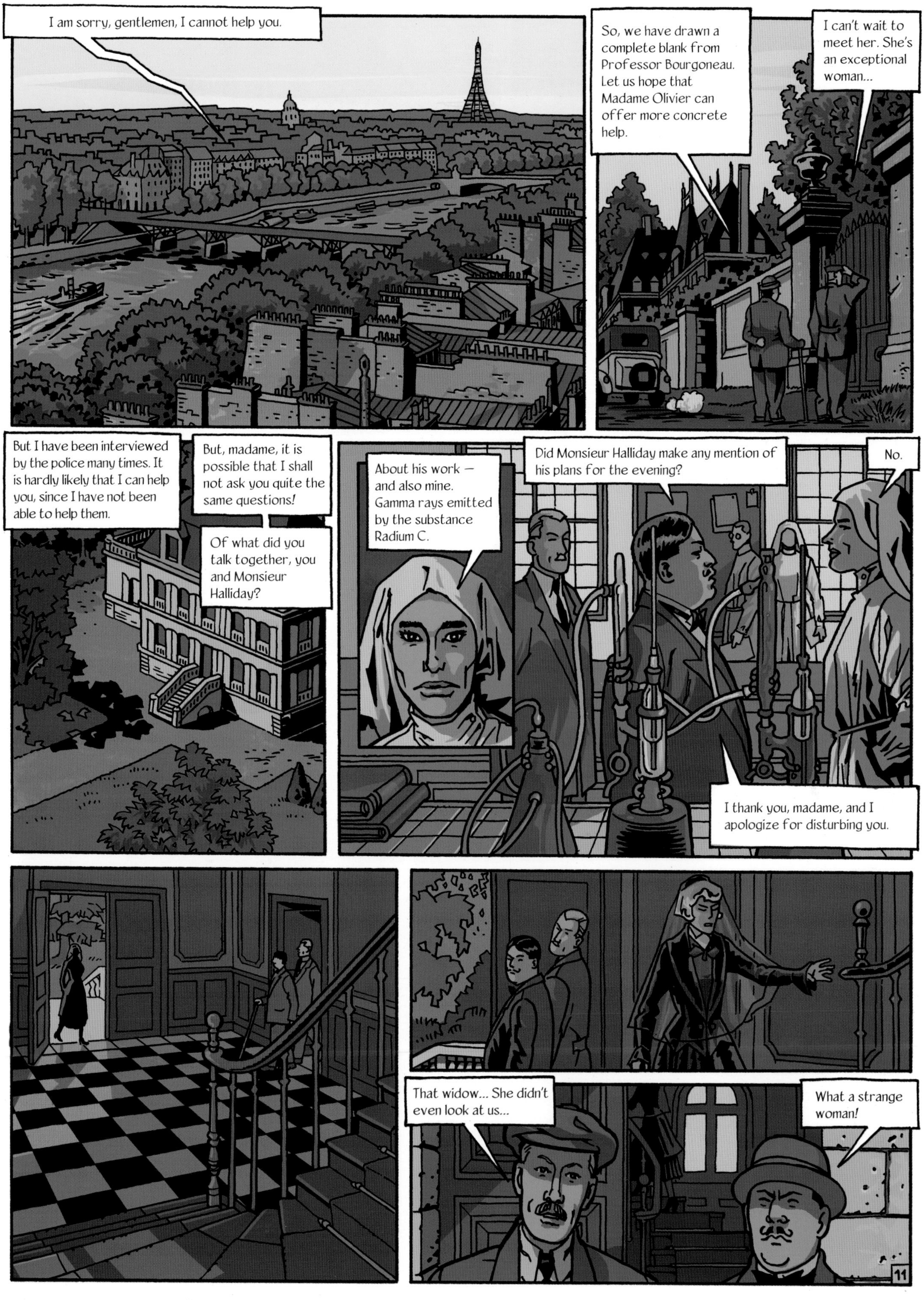
I am sorry, gentlemen, I cannot help you.
So, we have drawn a complete blank from Professor Bourgoneau. Let us hope that Madame Olivier can offer more concrete help.
I can't wait to meet her. She's an exceptional woman...
But I have been interviewed by the police many times. It is hardly likely that I can help you, since I have not been able to help them.
But, madame, it is possible that I shall not ask you quite the same questions!
Of what did you talk together, you and Monsieur Halliday?
About his work — and also mine. Gamma rays emitted by the substance Radium C.
Did Monsieur Halliday make any mention of his plans for the evening?
No.
I thank you, madame, and I apologize for disturbing you.
That widow... She didn't even look at us...
What a strange woman!
11

That perfume...?

Poirot, what are you doing?

Hush! I'm following my nose!

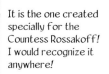

It is the one created specially for the Countess Rossakoff! I would recognize it anywhere!

Halliday doesn't know anything!

Listen to me! I've just seen Hercule Poirot! I must leave...

I'll see you later!

I have heard everything, Countess Rossakoff! Please may we come in?

I must ask you not to tell Madame Olivier about me.

I will make a bargain with you: freedom for me — and Mr Halliday, alive and well, for you.

I accept.

The little Belgian knows everything! Bring Halliday back to the hotel.

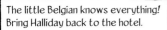
"The little Belgian"?!

You will accompany us, madame!

Monsieur Poirot, a gentleman has arrived. He is in your rooms.

Are you John Halliday?

We know that you have been kidnapped by the Big Four. What can you tell us about them?

Please don't make me talk about them! They have threatened the lives of my family!

Yes, it is I...

Countess, you are free to go.

13

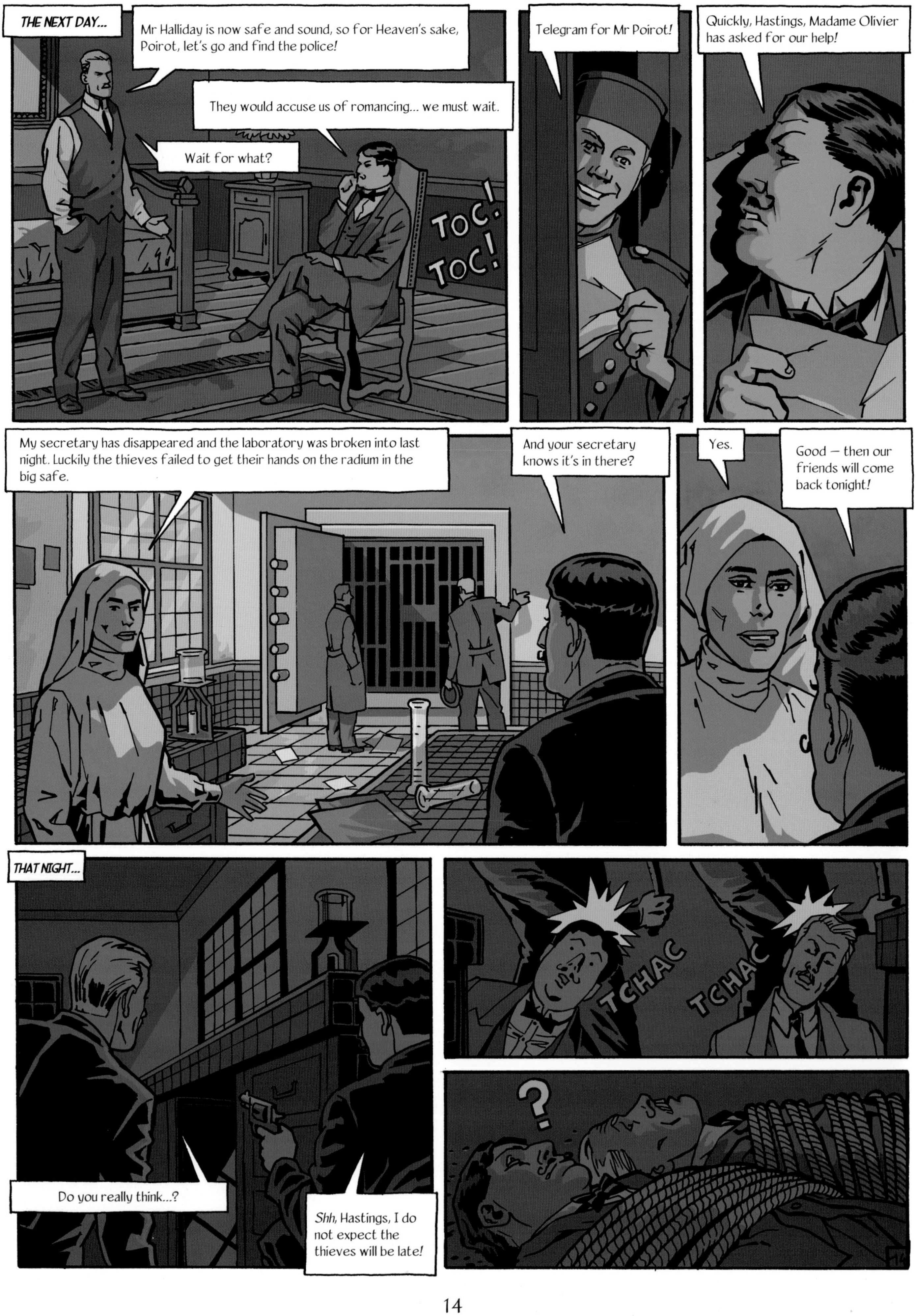
THE NEXT DAY...
Mr Halliday is now safe and sound, so for Heaven's sake, Poirot, let's go and find the police!
They would accuse us of romancing... we must wait.
Wait for what?
TOC! TOC!
Telegram for Mr Poirot!
Quickly, Hastings, Madame Olivier has asked for our help!
My secretary has disappeared and the laboratory was broken into last night. Luckily the thieves failed to get their hands on the radium in the big safe.
And your secretary knows it's in there?
Yes.
Good — then our friends will come back tonight!
THAT NIGHT...
Do you really think...?
Shh, Hastings, I do not expect the thieves will be late!
TCHAC
TCHAC
?

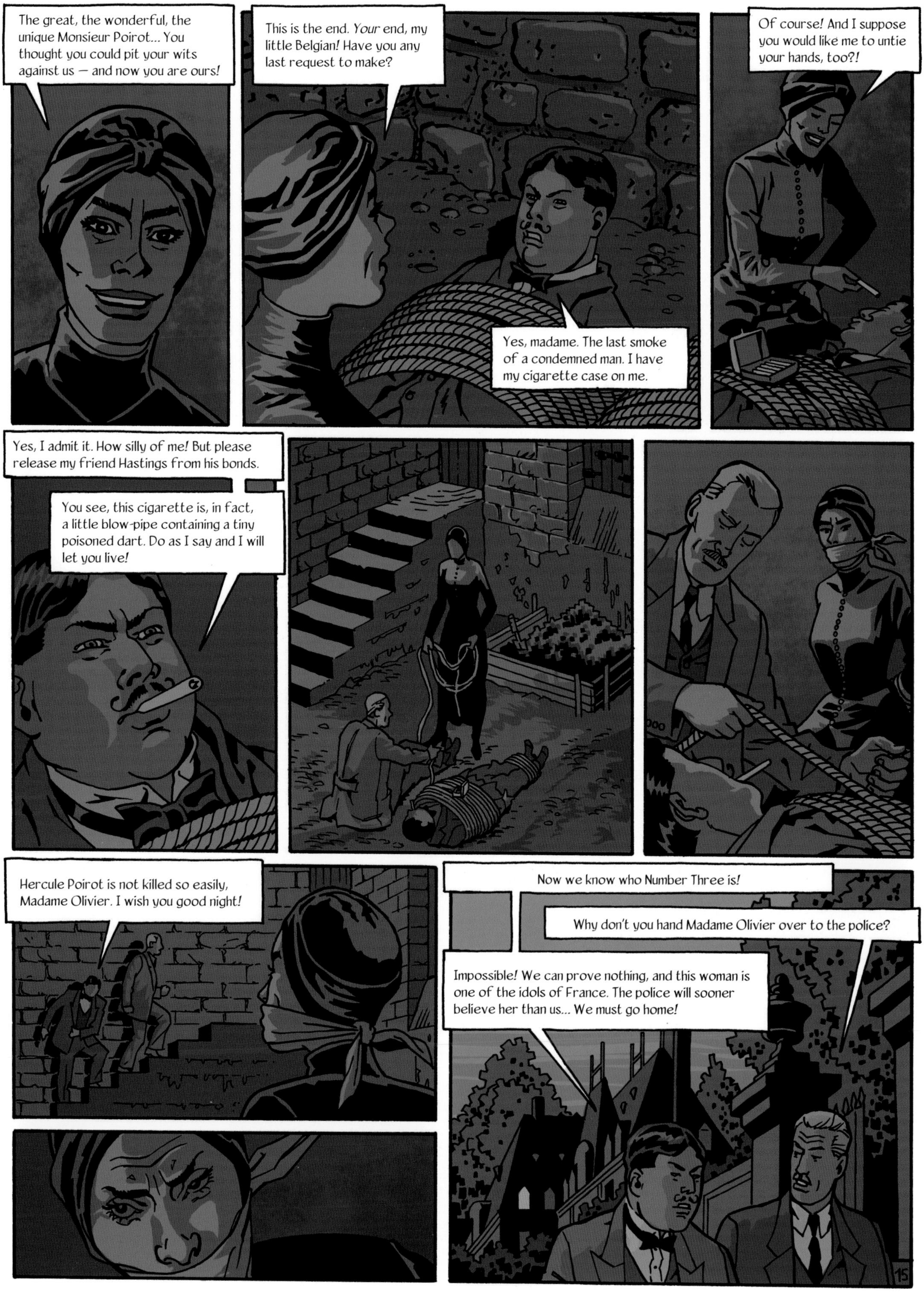
The great, the wonderful, the unique Monsieur Poirot... You thought you could pit your wits against us — and now you are ours!
This is the end. *Your* end, my little Belgian! Have you any last request to make?
Yes, madame. The last smoke of a condemned man. I have my cigarette case on me.
Of course! And I suppose you would like me to untie your hands, too?!
Yes, I admit it. How silly of me! But please release my friend Hastings from his bonds.
You see, this cigarette is, in fact, a little blow-pipe containing a tiny poisoned dart. Do as I say and I will let you live!
Hercule Poirot is not killed so easily, Madame Olivier. I wish you good night!
Now we know who Number Three is!
Why don't you hand Madame Olivier over to the police?
Impossible! We can prove nothing, and this woman is one of the idols of France. The police will sooner believe her than us... We must go home!

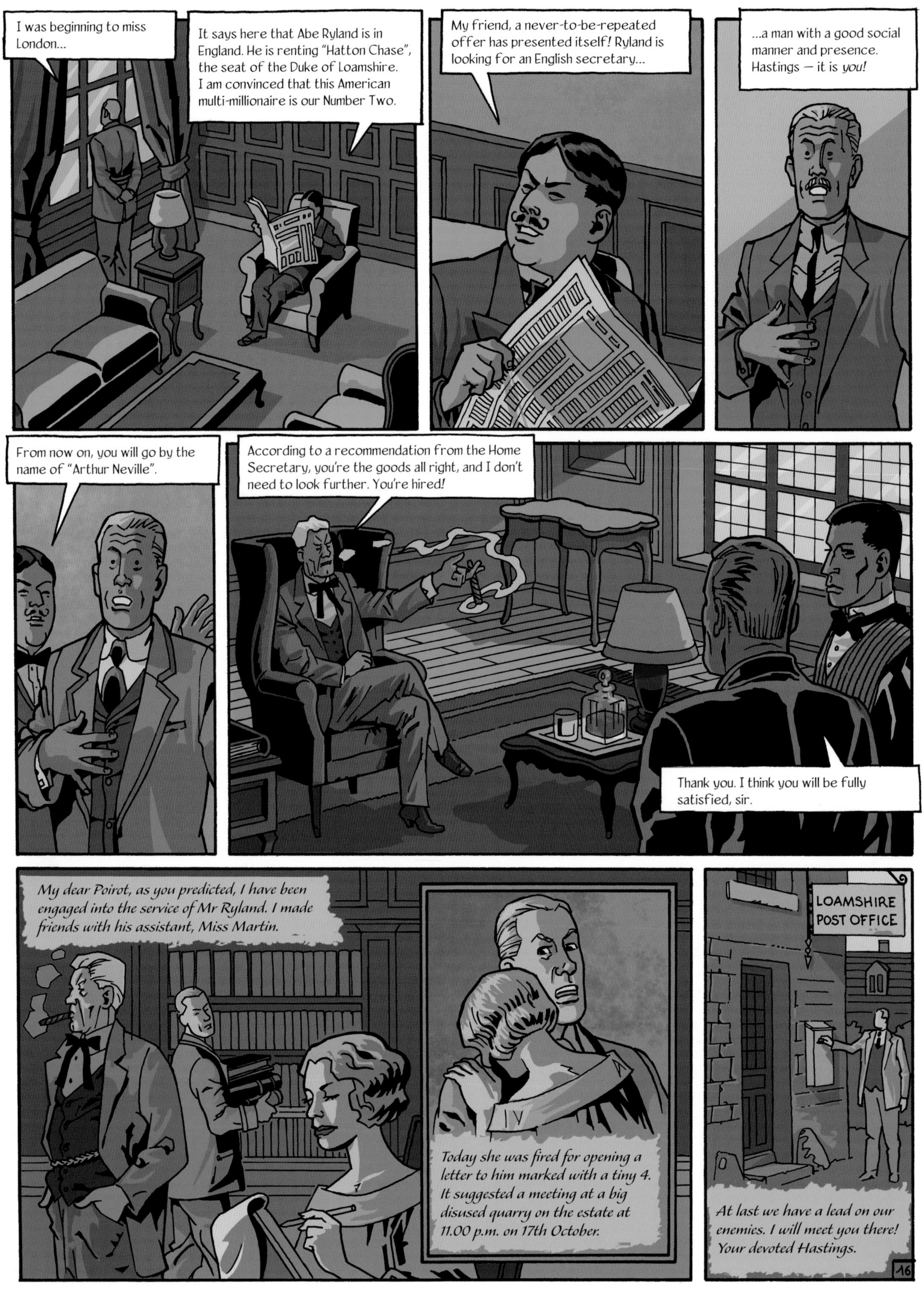
I was beginning to miss London...
It says here that Abe Ryland is in England. He is renting "Hatton Chase", the seat of the Duke of Loamshire. I am convinced that this American multi-millionaire is our Number Two.
My friend, a never-to-be-repeated offer has presented itself! Ryland is looking for an English secretary...
...a man with a good social manner and presence. Hastings — it is *you!*
From now on, you will go by the name of "Arthur Neville".
According to a recommendation from the Home Secretary, you're the goods all right, and I don't need to look further. You're hired!
Thank you. I think you will be fully satisfied, sir.
My dear Poirot, as you predicted, I have been engaged into the service of Mr Ryland. I made friends with his assistant, Miss Martin.
IV
Today she was fired for opening a letter to him marked with a tiny 4. It suggested a meeting at a big disused quarry on the estate at 11.00 p.m. on 17th October.
LOAMSHIRE POST OFFICE
At last we have a lead on our enemies. I will meet you there! Your devoted Hastings.
16

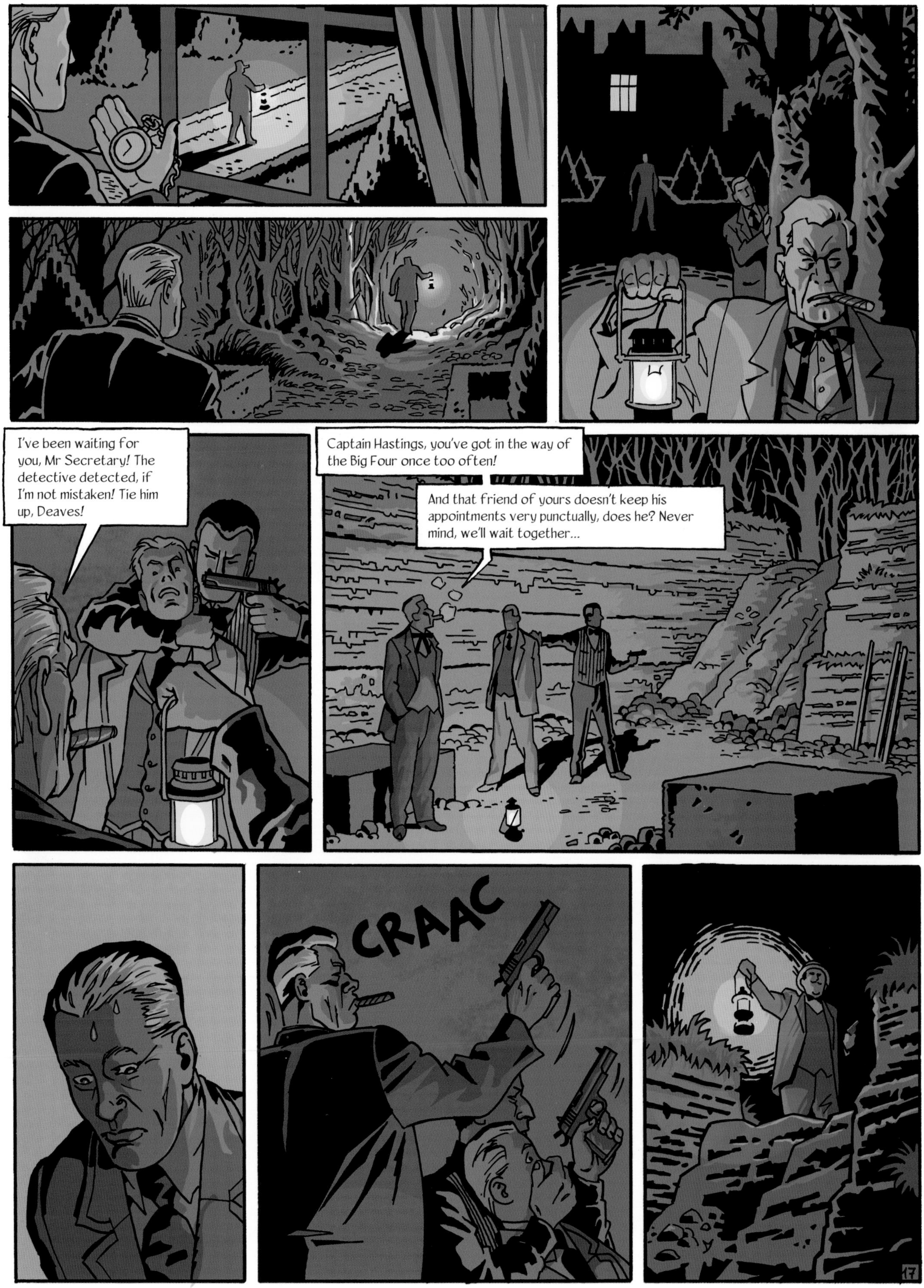
I've been waiting for you, Mr Secretary! The detective detected, if I'm not mistaken! Tie him up, Deaves!
Captain Hastings, you've got in the way of the Big Four once too often!
And that friend of yours doesn't keep his appointments very punctually, does he? Never mind, we'll wait together...
CRAAC

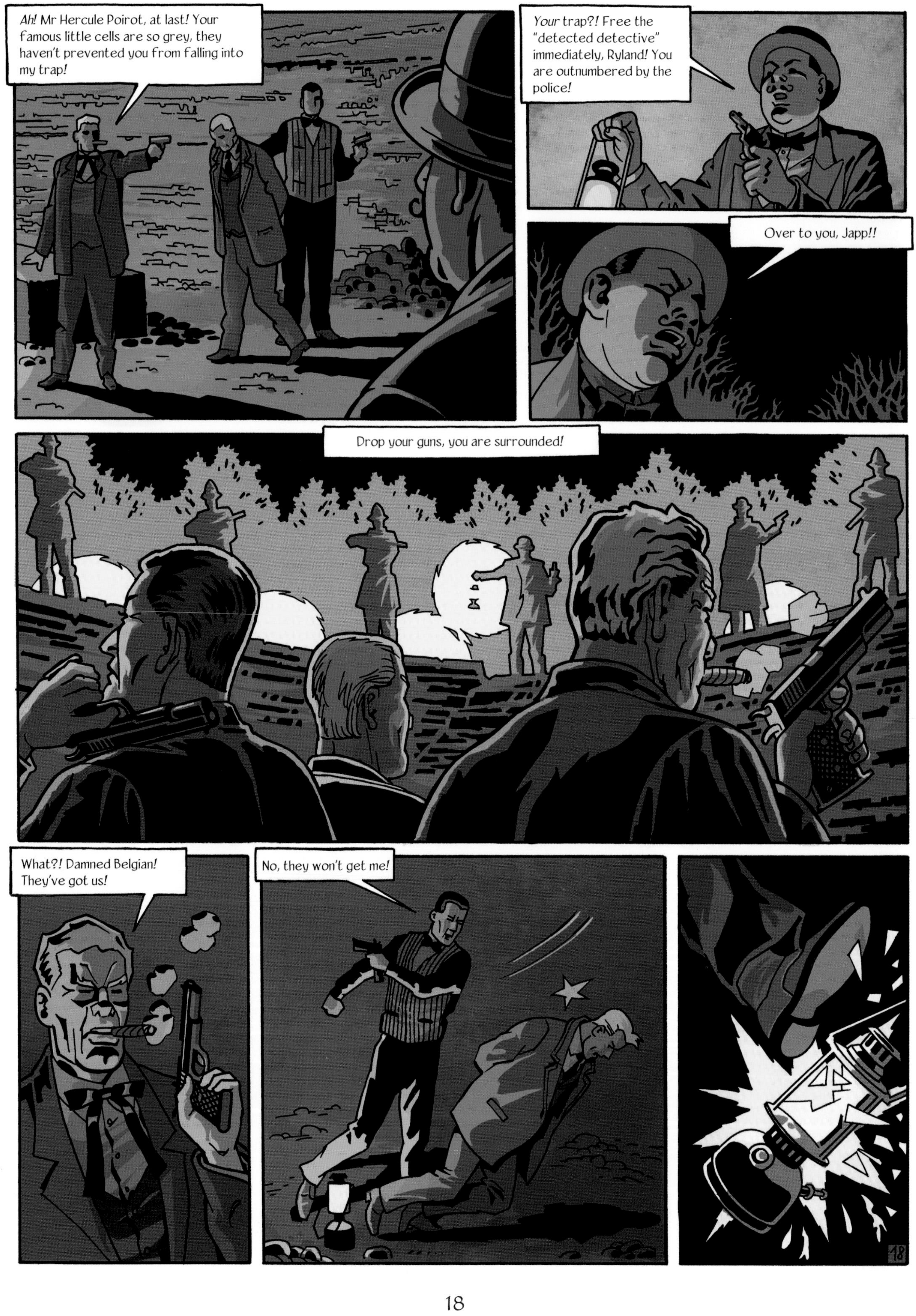
Ah! Mr Hercule Poirot, at last! Your famous little cells are so grey, they haven't prevented you from falling into my trap!
Your trap?! Free the "detected detective" immediately, Ryland! You are outnumbered by the police!
Over to you, Japp!!
Drop your guns, you are surrounded!
What?! Damned Belgian! They've got us!
No, they won't get me!

Don't shoot! You might hit Captain Hastings!

My dear friend, thank God! You are safe! These men are ruthless, they were going to kill you there and then!

So, Number Two of the Big Four is Abe Ryland. As for Deaves, the footman, that was a masquerade. He was Number Four!

Pleased to see you alive, Hastings!

Thank you for your help, Japp. Without you...

All part of the job, *Moosior* Poirot. What do you hope to do about Ryland?

The next time, as I know there will be one, it will be vital for us to act even more swiftly!

Nothing, alas! Abe Ryland is much too powerful to let this worry him.

And we still have no proof! Even you, in this darkness, could not swear to have recognized him, and no doubt a dozen servants in his household will vouch that he did not leave his room all evening...

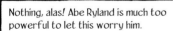

19

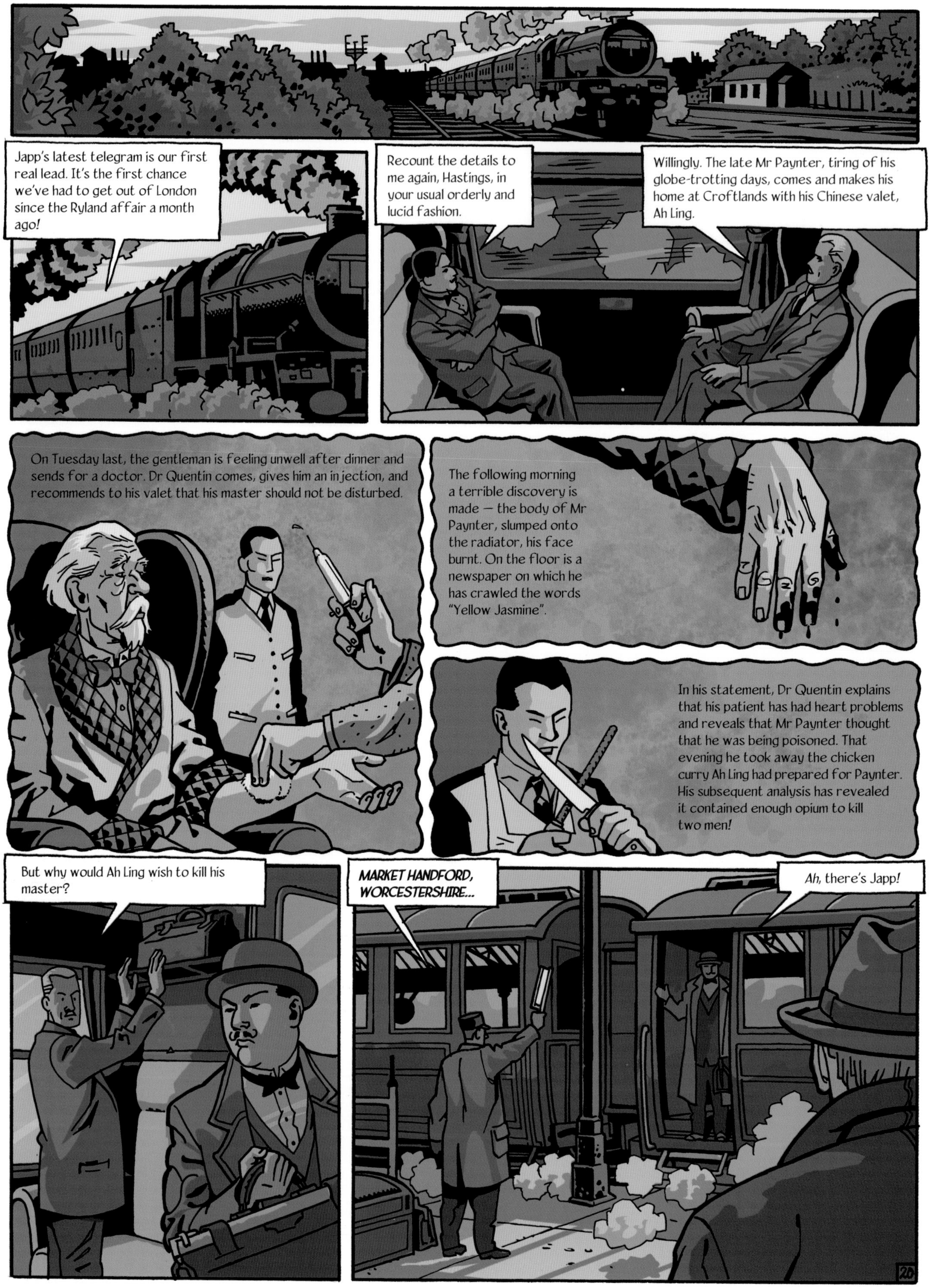

Japp's latest telegram is our first real lead. It's the first chance we've had to get out of London since the Ryland affair a month ago!
Recount the details to me again, Hastings, in your usual orderly and lucid fashion.
Willingly. The late Mr Paynter, tiring of his globe-trotting days, comes and makes his home at Croftlands with his Chinese valet, Ah Ling.
On Tuesday last, the gentleman is feeling unwell after dinner and sends for a doctor. Dr Quentin comes, gives him an injection, and recommends to his valet that his master should not be disturbed.
The following morning a terrible discovery is made — the body of Mr Paynter, slumped onto the radiator, his face burnt. On the floor is a newspaper on which he has crawled the words "Yellow Jasmine".
In his statement, Dr Quentin explains that his patient has had heart problems and reveals that Mr Paynter thought that he was being poisoned. That evening he took away the chicken curry Ah Ling had prepared for Paynter. His subsequent analysis has revealed it contained enough opium to kill two men!
But why would Ah Ling wish to kill his master?
MARKET HANDFORD, WORCESTERSHIRE...
Ah, there's Japp!
20

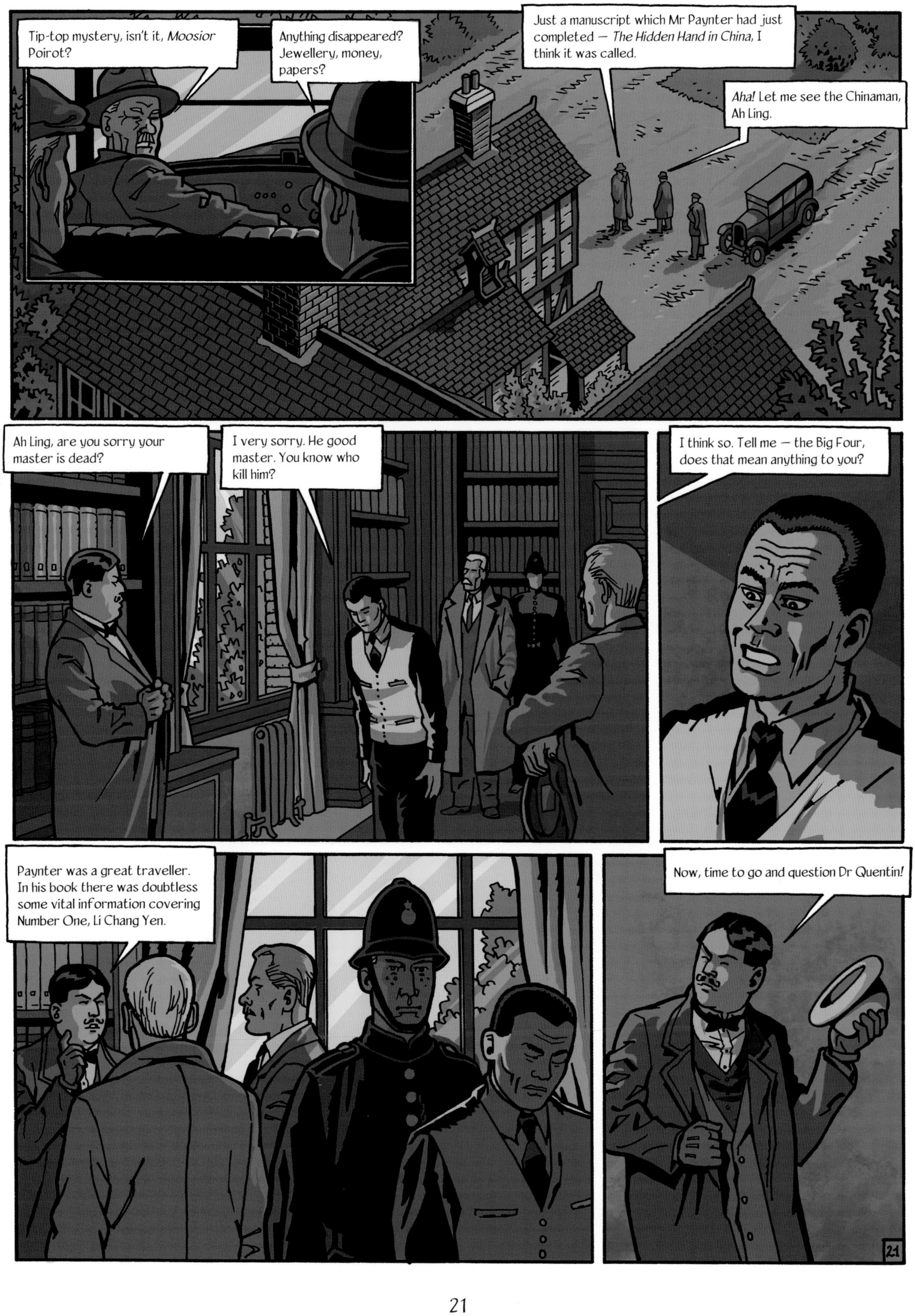
Tip-top mystery, isn't it, *Moosior* Poirot?
Anything disappeared? Jewellery, money, papers?
Just a manuscript which Mr Paynter had just completed — *The Hidden Hand in China*, I think it was called.
Aha! Let me see the Chinaman, Ah Ling.
Ah Ling, are you sorry your master is dead?
I very sorry. He good master. You know who kill him?
I think so. Tell me — the Big Four, does that mean anything to you?
Paynter was a great traveller. In his book there was doubtless some vital information covering Number One, Li Chang Yen.
Now, time to go and question Dr Quentin!
21

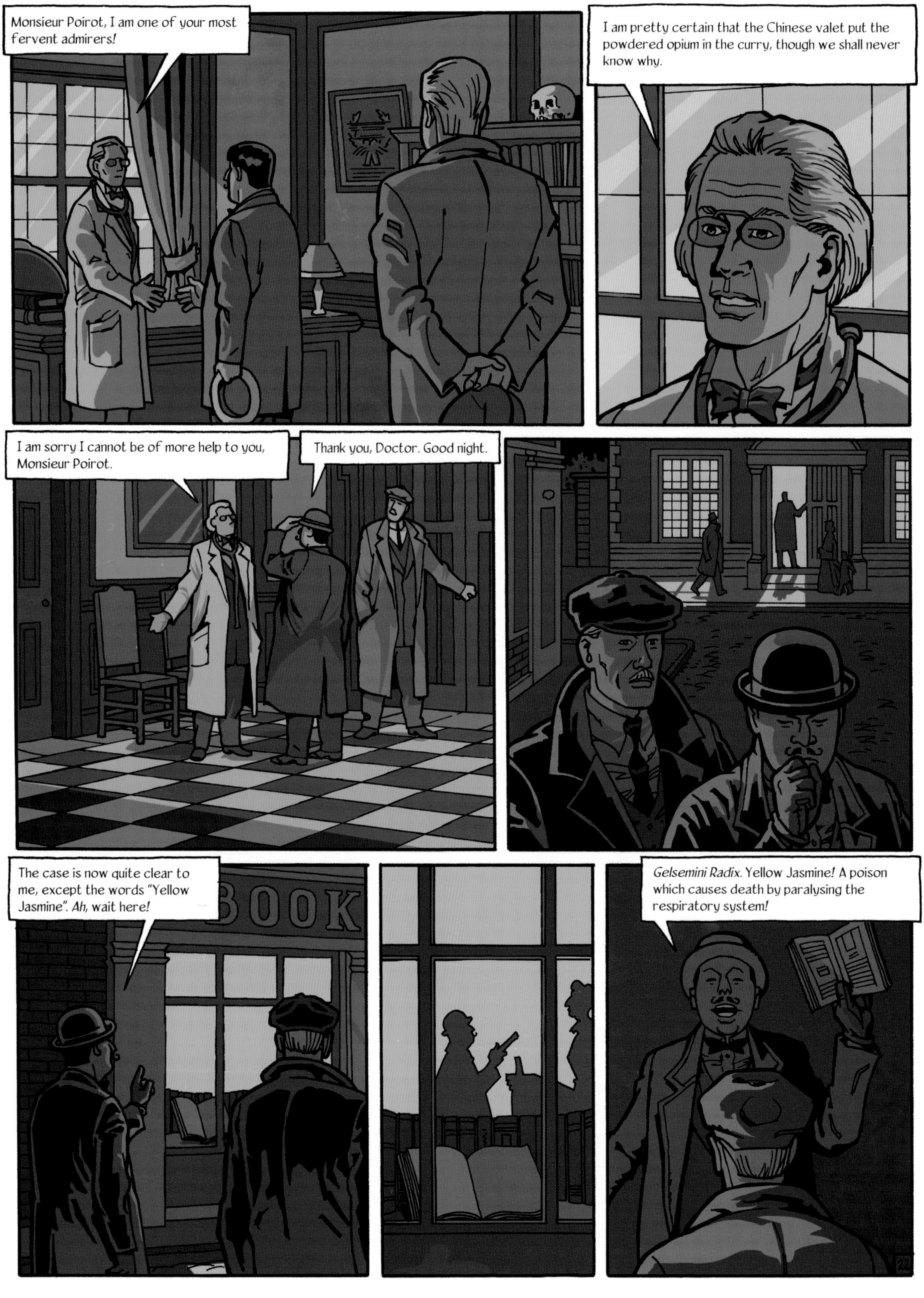
Monsieur Poirot, I am one of your most fervent admirers!
I am pretty certain that the Chinese valet put the powdered opium in the curry, though we shall never know why.
I am sorry I cannot be of more help to you, Monsieur Poirot.
Thank you, Doctor. Good night.
The case is now quite clear to me, except the words "Yellow Jasmine". Ah, wait here!
BOOK
Gelsemini Radix. Yellow Jasmine! A poison which causes death by paralysing the respiratory system!

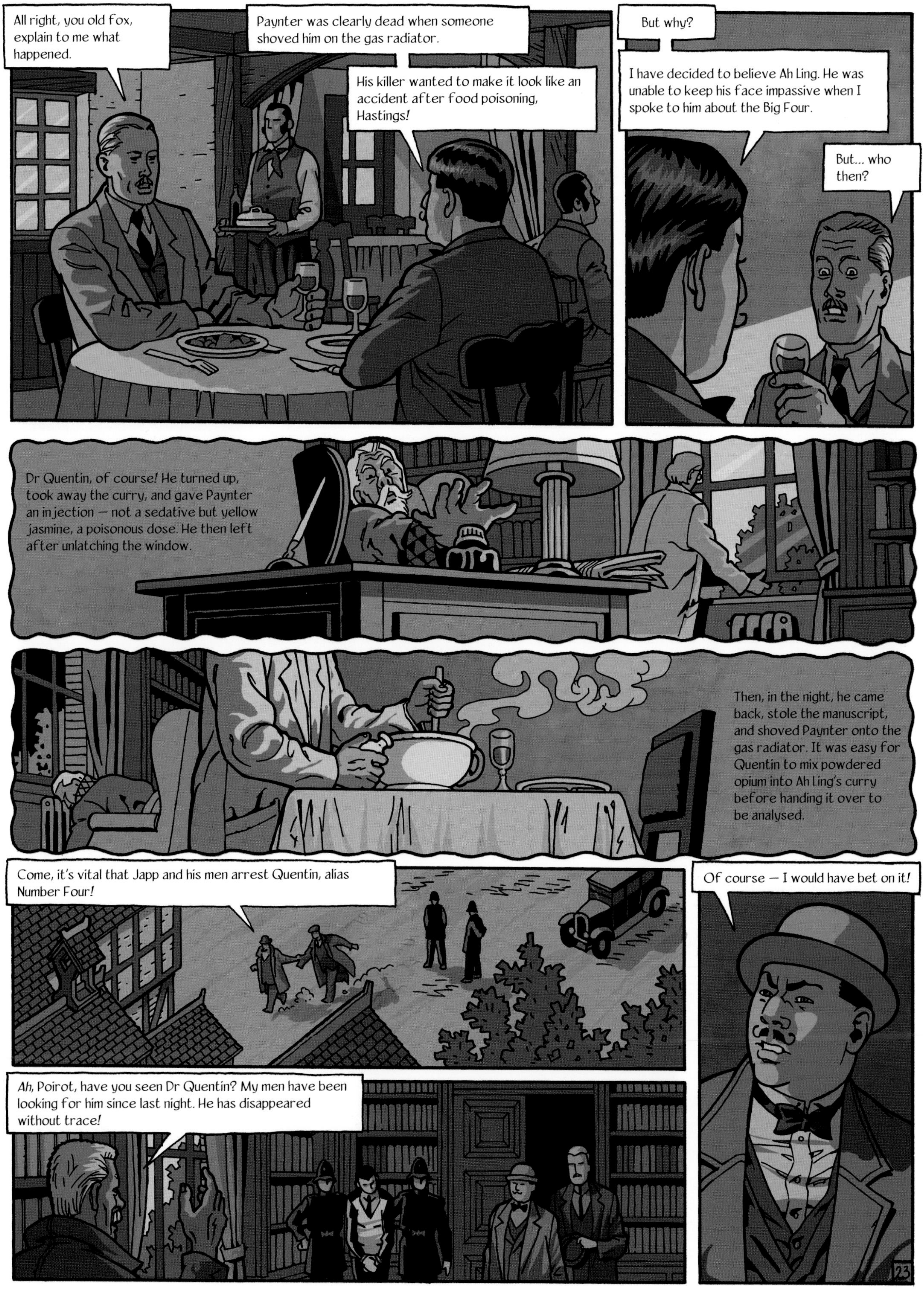
All right, you old fox, explain to me what happened.
Paynter was clearly dead when someone shoved him on the gas radiator.
His killer wanted to make it look like an accident after food poisoning, Hastings!
But why?
I have decided to believe Ah Ling. He was unable to keep his face impassive when I spoke to him about the Big Four.
But... who then?
Dr Quentin, of course! He turned up, took away the curry, and gave Paynter an injection — not a sedative but yellow jasmine, a poisonous dose. He then left after unlatching the window.
Then, in the night, he came back, stole the manuscript, and shoved Paynter onto the gas radiator. It was easy for Quentin to mix powdered opium into Ah Ling's curry before handing it over to be analysed.
Come, it's vital that Japp and his men arrest Quentin, alias Number Four!
Of course — I would have bet on it!
Ah, Poirot, have you seen Dr Quentin? My men have been looking for him since last night. He has disappeared without trace!
23

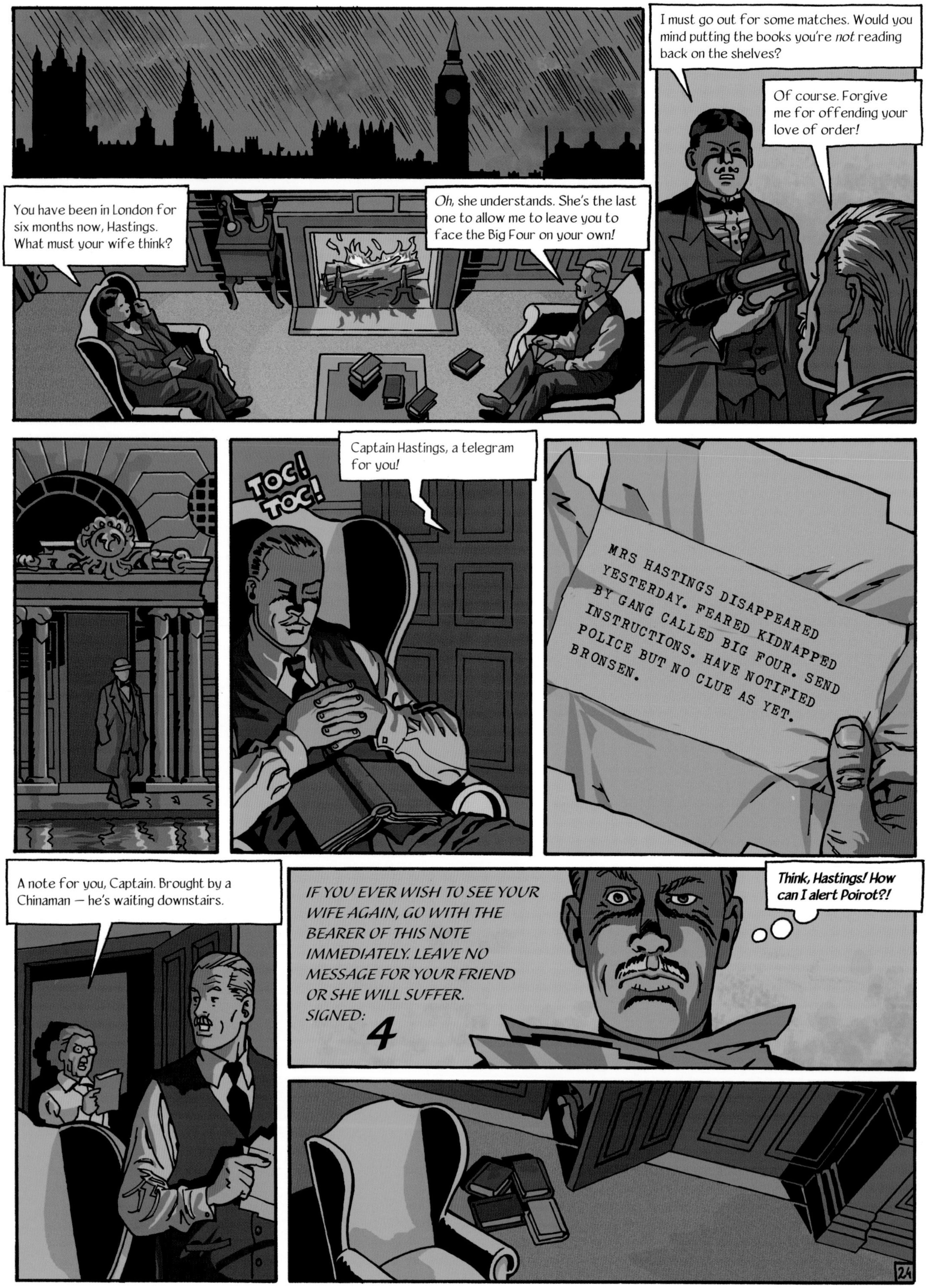
I must go out for some matches. Would you mind putting the books you're *not* reading back on the shelves?
You have been in London for six months now, Hastings. What must your wife think?
Oh, she understands. She's the last one to allow me to leave you to face the Big Four on your own!
Of course. Forgive me for offending your love of order!
TOC! TOC!
Captain Hastings, a telegram for you!
MRS HASTINGS DISAPPEARED YESTERDAY. FEARED KIDNAPPED BY GANG CALLED BIG FOUR. SEND INSTRUCTIONS. HAVE NOTIFIED POLICE BUT NO CLUE AS YET. BRONSEN.
A note for you, Captain. Brought by a Chinaman — he's waiting downstairs.
IF YOU EVER WISH TO SEE YOUR WIFE AGAIN, GO WITH THE BEARER OF THIS NOTE IMMEDIATELY. LEAVE NO MESSAGE FOR YOUR FRIEND OR SHE WILL SUFFER. SIGNED: 4
Think, Hastings! How can I alert Poirot?!
24

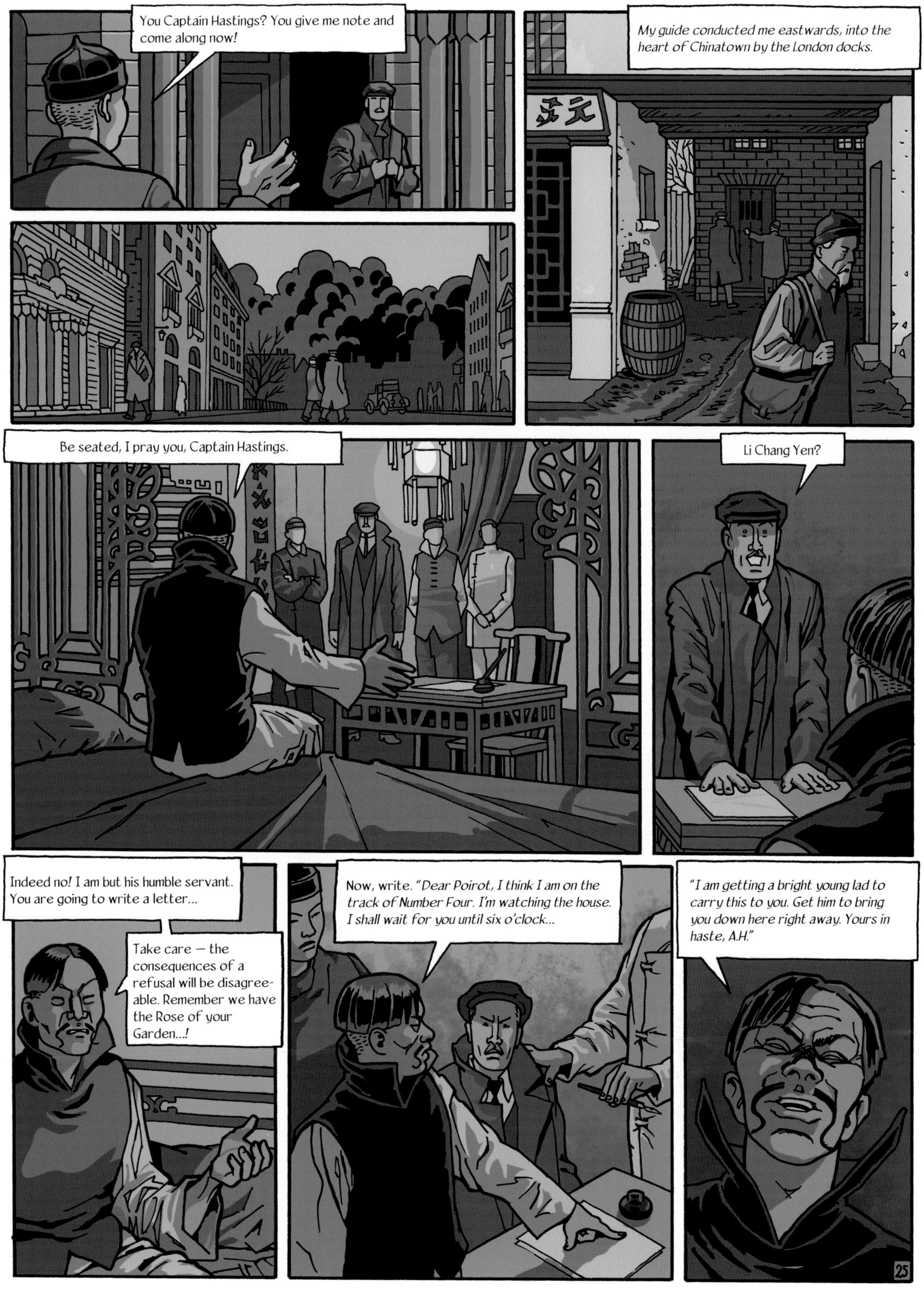
You Captain Hastings? You give me note and come along now!
My guide conducted me eastwards, into the heart of Chinatown by the London docks.
Be seated, I pray you, Captain Hastings.
Li Chang Yen?
Indeed no! I am but his humble servant. You are going to write a letter...
Take care — the consequences of a refusal will be disagreeable. Remember we have the Rose of your Garden...!
Now, write. "Dear Poirot, I think I am on the track of Number Four. I'm watching the house. I shall wait for you until six o'clock...
"I am getting a bright young lad to carry this to you. Get him to bring you down here right away. Yours in haste, A.H."
25

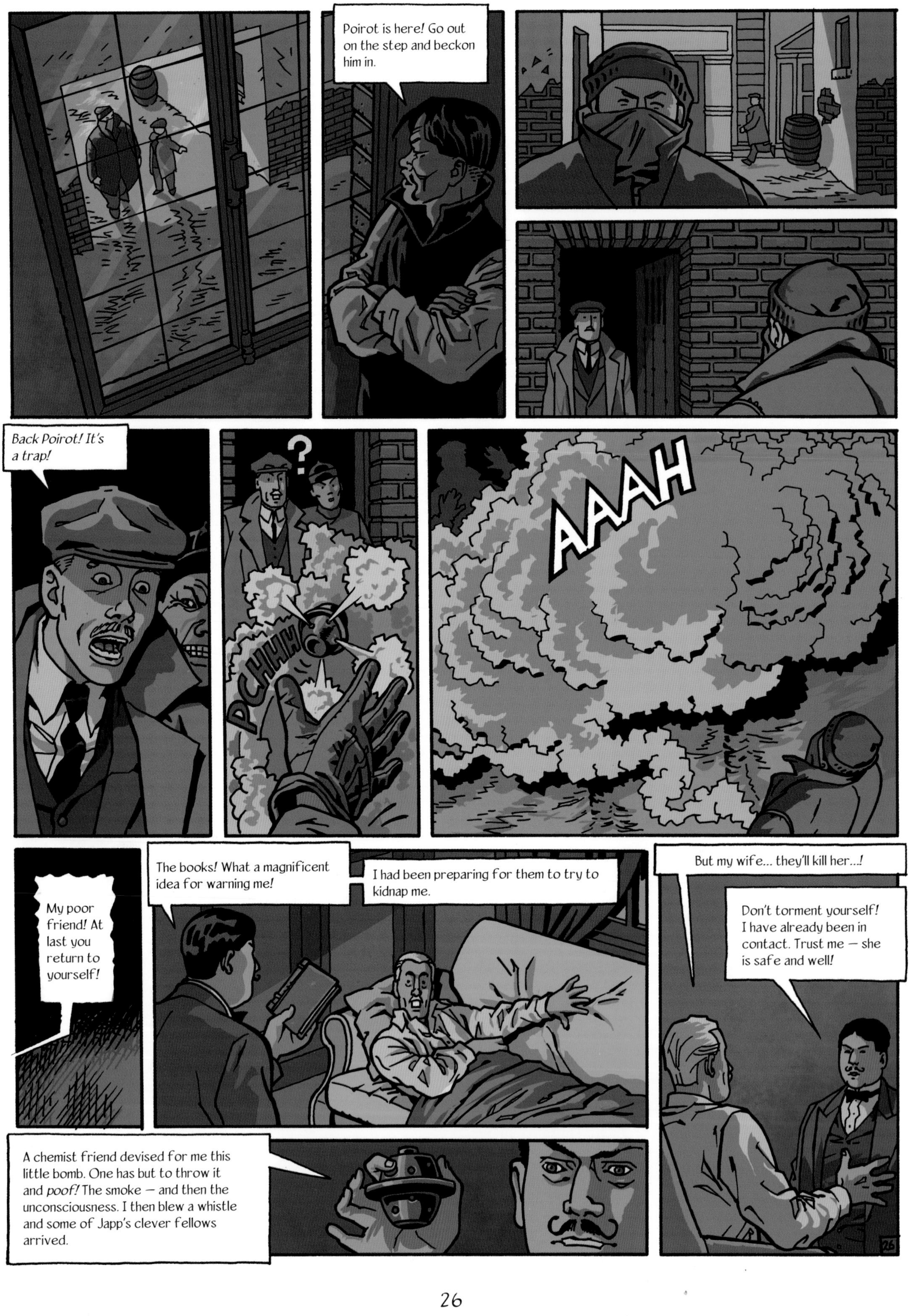
Poirot is here! Go out on the step and beckon him in.
Back Poirot! It's a trap!
?
PCHHH
AAAH
My poor friend! At last you return to yourself!
The books! What a magnificent idea for warning me!
I had been preparing for them to try to kidnap me.
But my wife... they'll kill her...!
Don't torment yourself! I have already been in contact. Trust me — she is safe and well!
A chemist friend devised for me this little bomb. One has but to throw it and *poof!* The smoke — and then the unconsciousness. I then blew a whistle and some of Japp's clever fellows arrived.
26

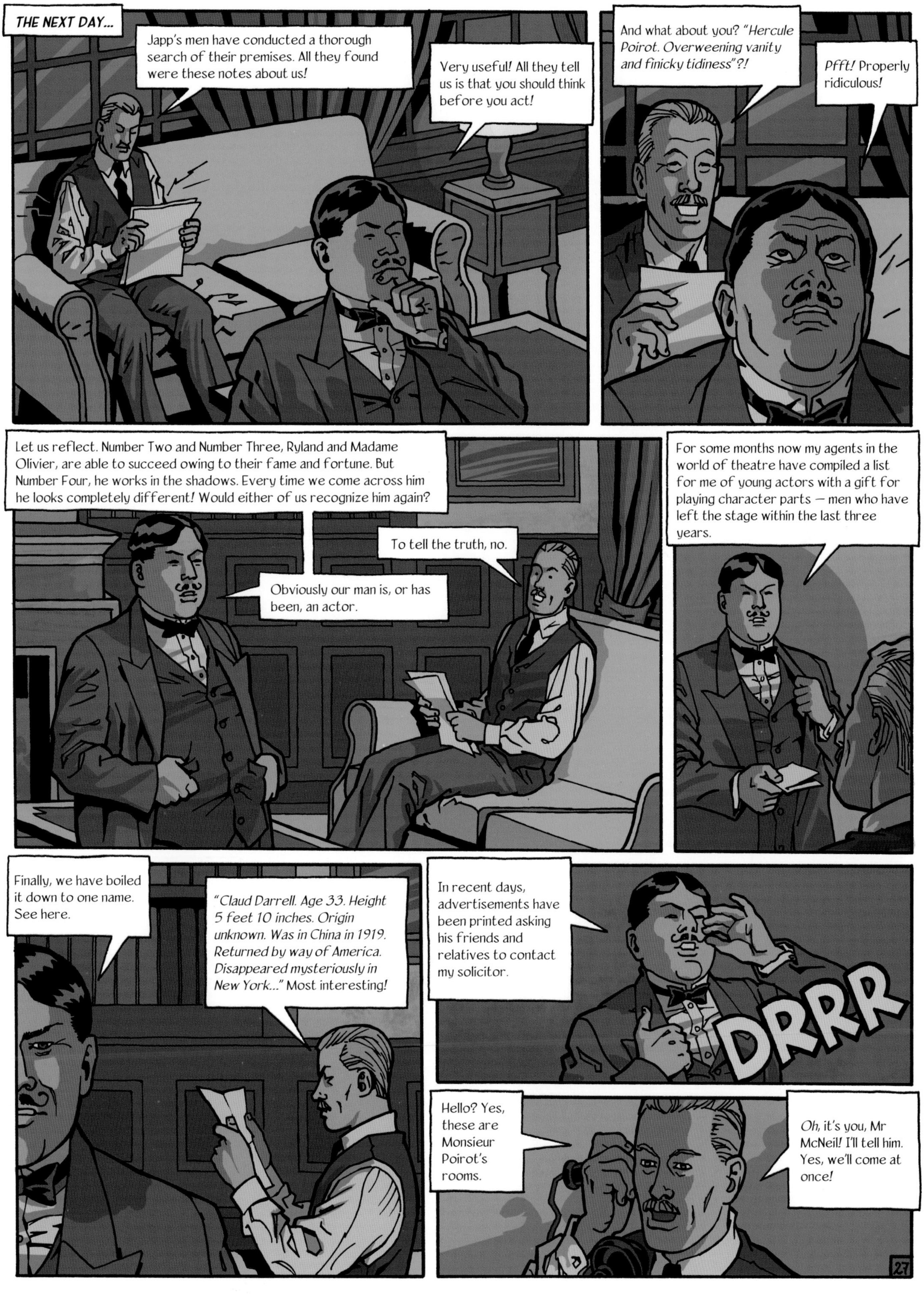
THE NEXT DAY...
Japp's men have conducted a thorough search of their premises. All they found were these notes about us!
Very useful! All they tell us is that you should think before you act!
And what about you? "Hercule Poirot. Overweening vanity and finicky tidiness"?!
Pfft! Properly ridiculous!
Let us reflect. Number Two and Number Three, Ryland and Madame Olivier, are able to succeed owing to their fame and fortune. But Number Four, he works in the shadows. Every time we come across him he looks completely different! Would either of us recognize him again?
To tell the truth, no.
Obviously our man is, or has been, an actor.
For some months now my agents in the world of theatre have compiled a list for me of young actors with a gift for playing character parts — men who have left the stage within the last three years.
Finally, we have boiled it down to one name. See here.
"Claud Darrell. Age 33. Height 5 feet 10 inches. Origin unknown. Was in China in 1919. Returned by way of America. Disappeared mysteriously in New York..." Most interesting!
In recent days, advertisements have been printed asking his friends and relatives to contact my solicitor.
DRRR
Hello? Yes, these are Monsieur Poirot's rooms.
Oh, it's you, Mr McNeil! I'll tell him. Yes, we'll come at once!
27

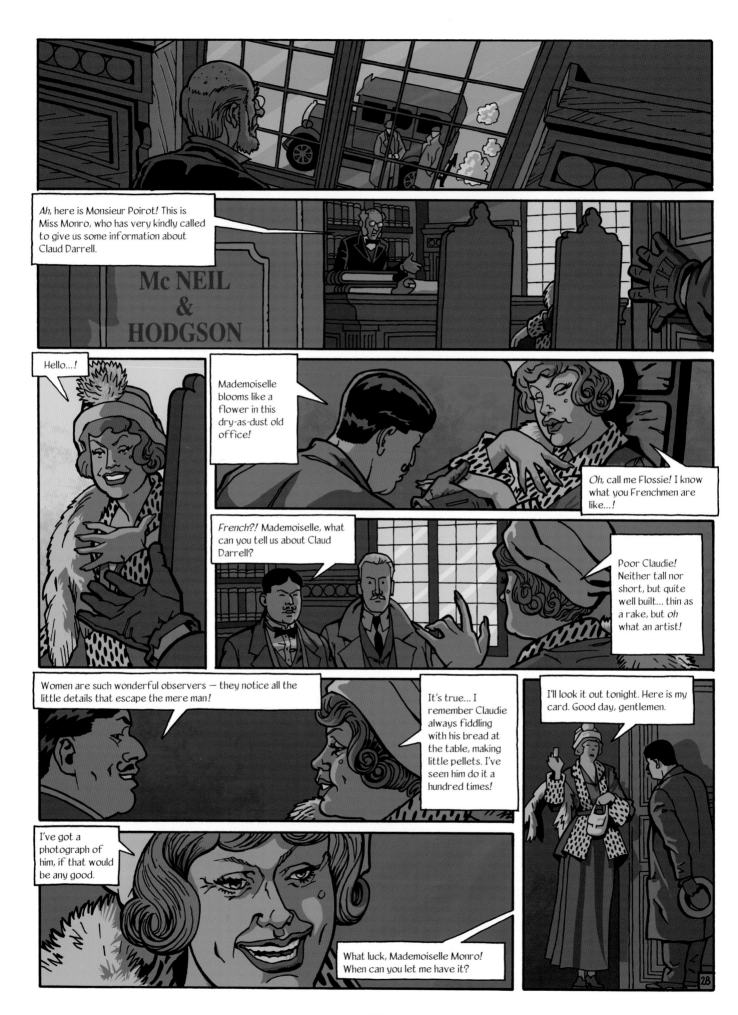

Ah, here is Monsieur Poirot! This is Miss Monro, who has very kindly called to give us some information about Claud Darrell.

Mc NEIL & HODGSON

Hello...!

Mademoiselle blooms like a flower in this dry-as-dust old office!

Oh, call me Flossie! I know what you Frenchmen are like...!

French?! Mademoiselle, what can you tell us about Claud Darrell?

Poor Claudie! Neither tall nor short, but quite well built... thin as a rake, but oh what an artist!

Women are such wonderful observers — they notice all the little details that escape the mere man!

It's true... I remember Claudie always fiddling with his bread at the table, making little pellets. I've seen him do it a hundred times!

I'll look it out tonight. Here is my card. Good day, gentlemen.

I've got a photograph of him, if that would be any good.

What luck, Mademoiselle Monro! When can you let me have it?

28

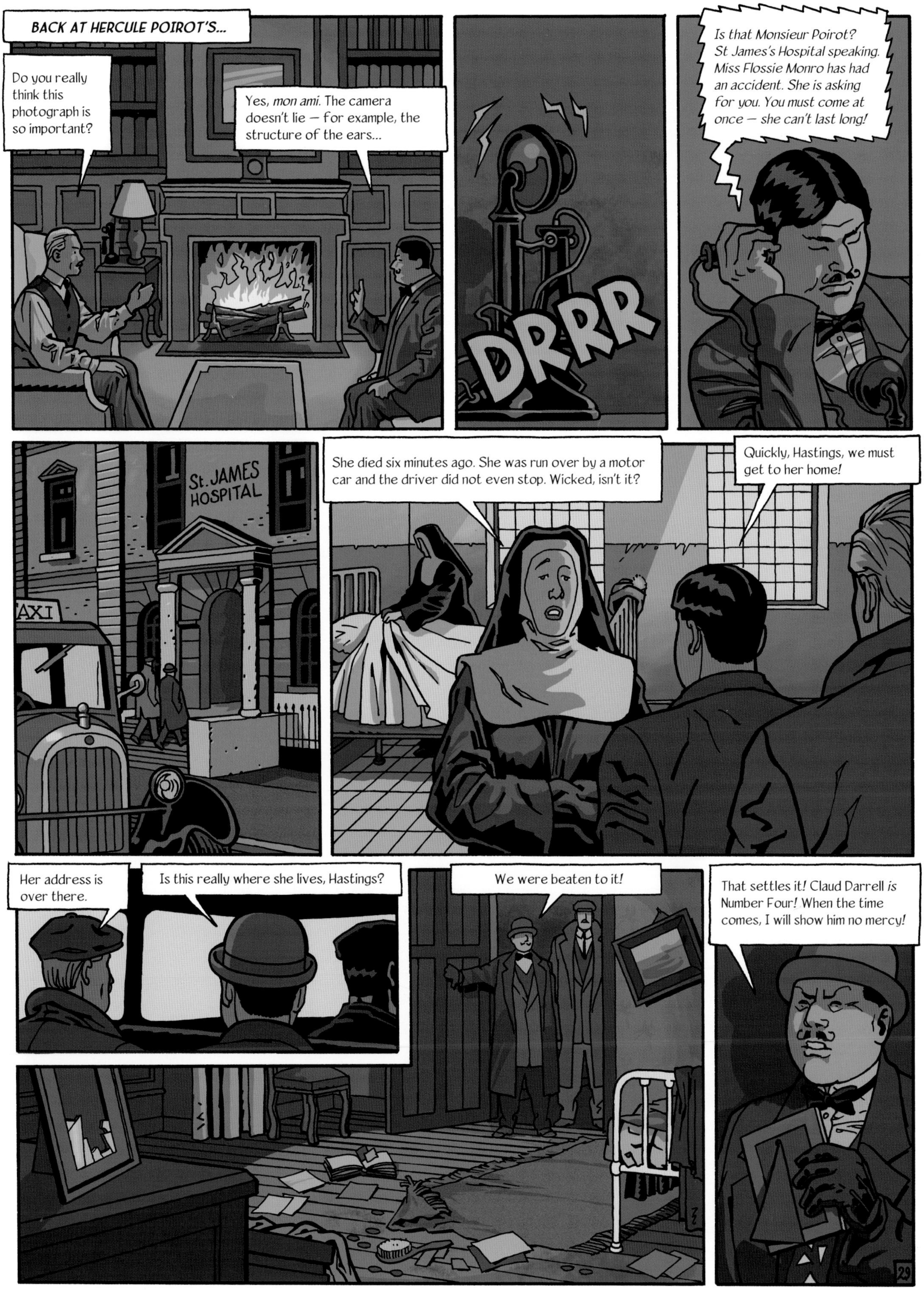
BACK AT HERCULE POIROT'S...
Do you really think this photograph is so important?
Yes, *mon ami*. The camera doesn't lie — for example, the structure of the ears...
DRRR
Is that Monsieur Poirot? St James's Hospital speaking. Miss Flossie Monro has had an accident. She is asking for you. You must come at once — she can't last long!
St. JAMES HOSPITAL
TAXI
She died six minutes ago. She was run over by a motor car and the driver did not even stop. Wicked, isn't it?
Quickly, Hastings, we must get to her home!
Her address is over there.
Is this really where she lives, Hastings?
We were beaten to it!
That settles it! Claud Darrell *is* Number Four! When the time comes, I will show him no mercy!
29

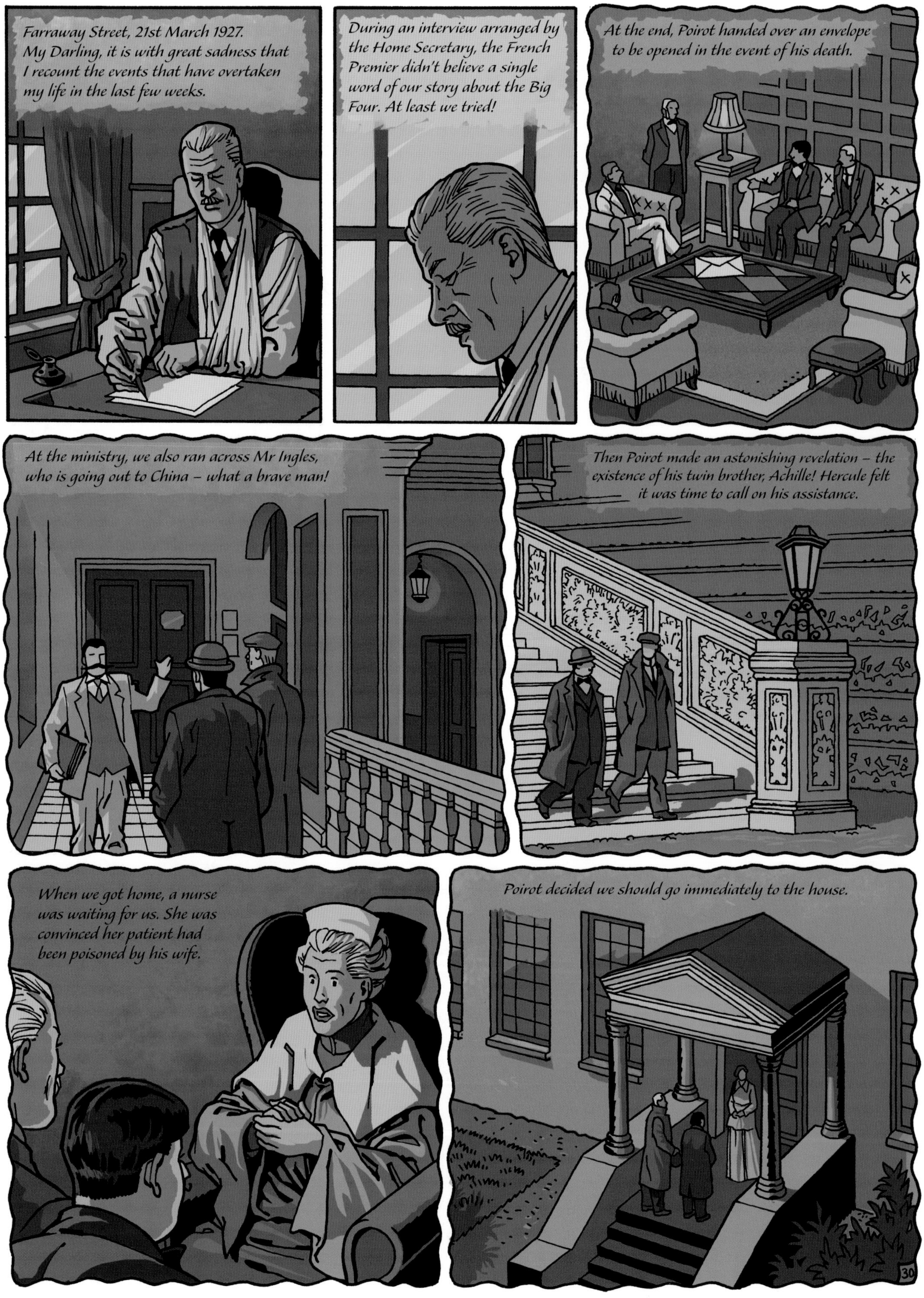
Farraway Street, 21st March 1927.
My Darling, it is with great sadness that I recount the events that have overtaken my life in the last few weeks.
During an interview arranged by the Home Secretary, the French Premier didn't believe a single word of our story about the Big Four. At least we tried!
At the end, Poirot handed over an envelope to be opened in the event of his death.
At the ministry, we also ran across Mr Ingles, who is going out to China – what a brave man!
Then Poirot made an astonishing revelation – the existence of his twin brother, Achille! Hercule felt it was time to call on his assistance.
When we got home, a nurse was waiting for us. She was convinced her patient had been poisoned by his wife.
Poirot decided we should go immediately to the house.
30

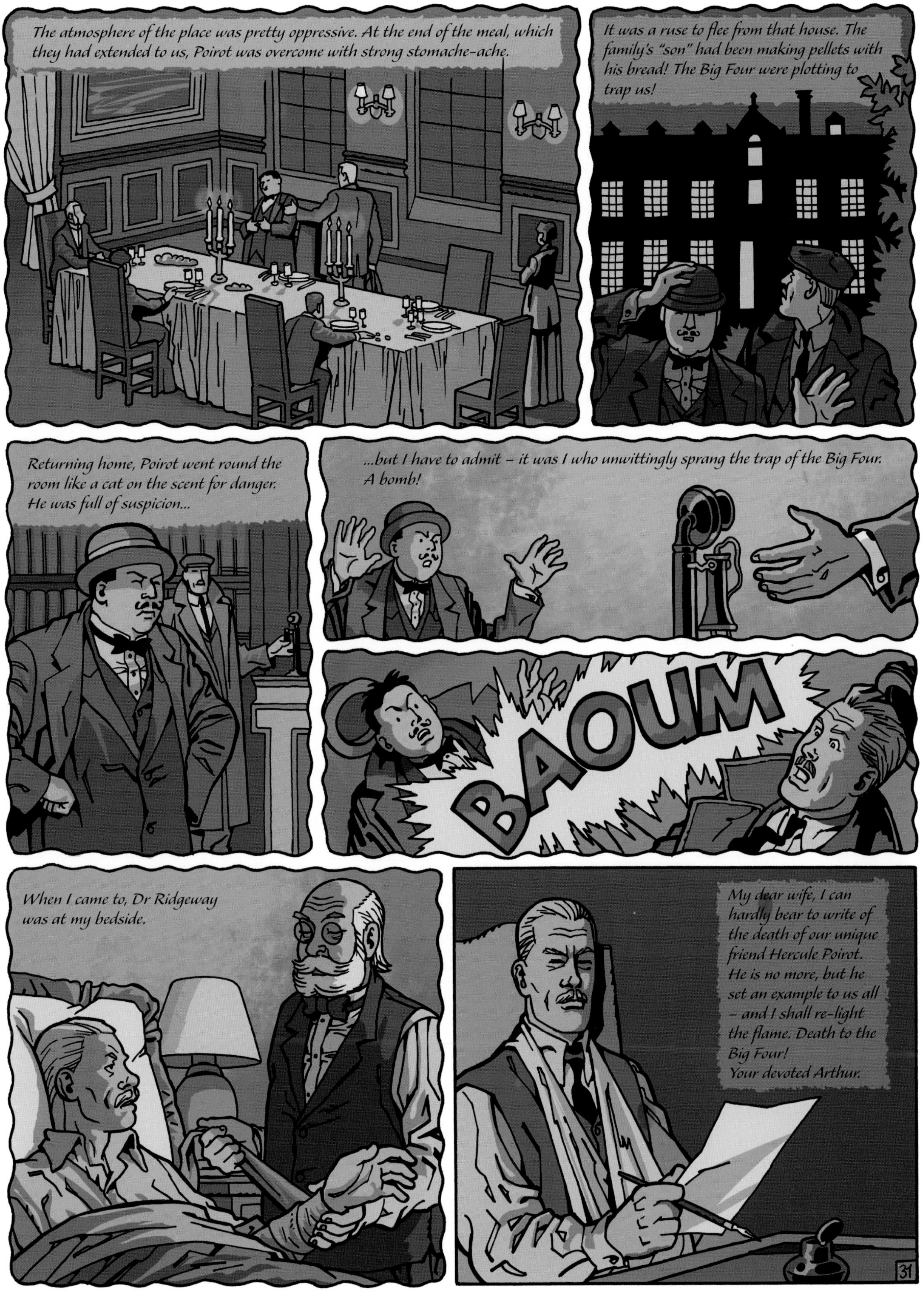
The atmosphere of the place was pretty oppressive. At the end of the meal, which they had extended to us, Poirot was overcome with strong stomache-ache.
It was a ruse to flee from that house. The family's "son" had been making pellets with his bread! The Big Four were plotting to trap us!
Returning home, Poirot went round the room like a cat on the scent for danger. He was full of suspicion...
...but I have to admit – it was I who unwittingly sprang the trap of the Big Four. A bomb!
BAOUM
When I came to, Dr Ridgeway was at my bedside.
My dear wife, I can hardly bear to write of the death of our unique friend Hercule Poirot. He is no more, but he set an example to us all – and I shall re-light the flame. Death to the Big Four! Your devoted Arthur.
31

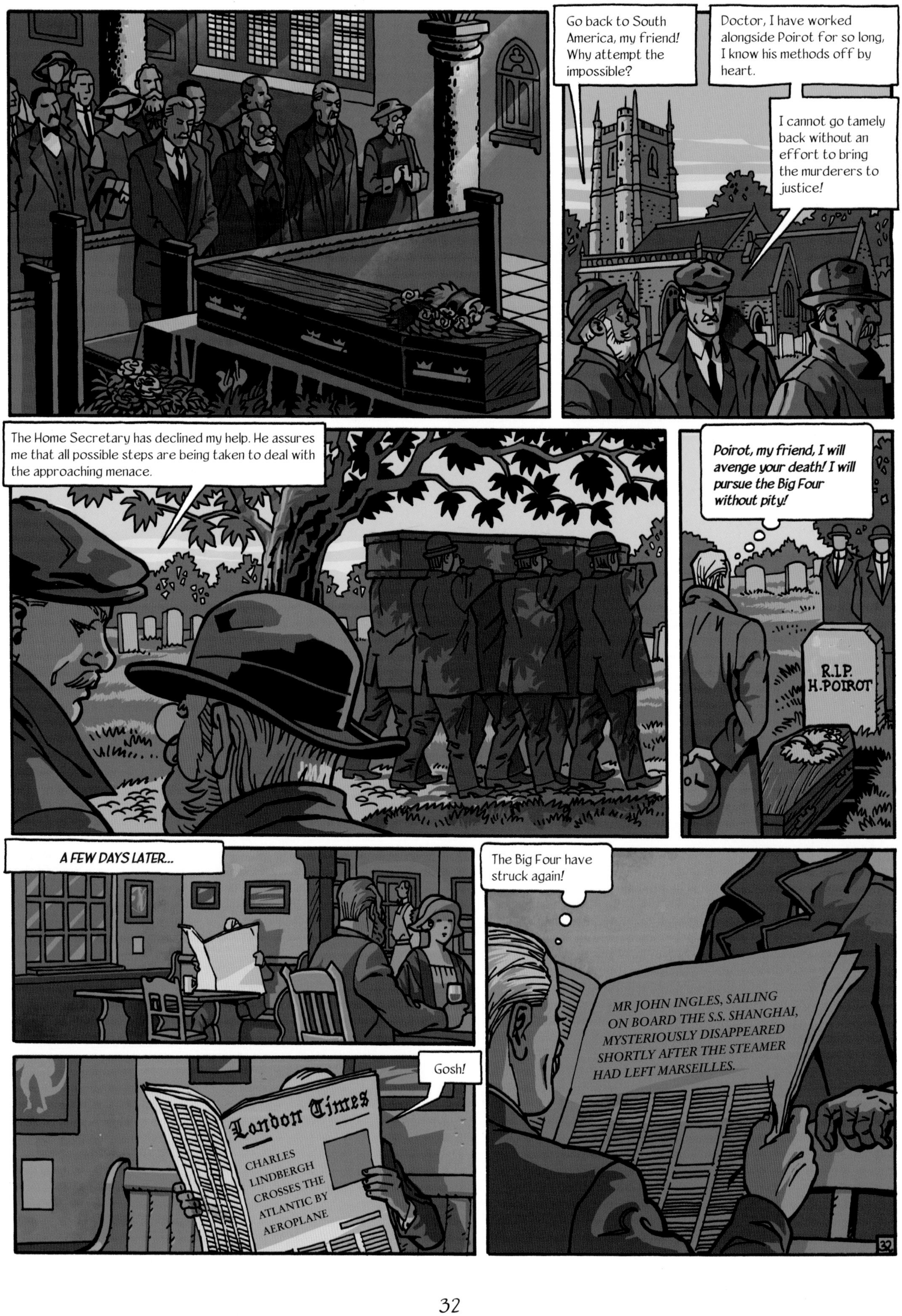

Go back to South America, my friend! Why attempt the impossible?
Doctor, I have worked alongside Poirot for so long, I know his methods off by heart.
I cannot go tamely back without an effort to bring the murderers to justice!
The Home Secretary has declined my help. He assures me that all possible steps are being taken to deal with the approaching menace.
Poirot, my friend, I will avenge your death! I will pursue the Big Four without pity!
R.I.P.
H. POIROT
A FEW DAYS LATER...
London Times
CHARLES LINDBERGH CROSSES THE ATLANTIC BY AEROPLANE
Gosh!
The Big Four have struck again!
MR JOHN INGLES, SAILING ON BOARD THE S.S. SHANGHAI, MYSTERIOUSLY DISAPPEARED SHORTLY AFTER THE STEAMER HAD LEFT MARSEILLES.

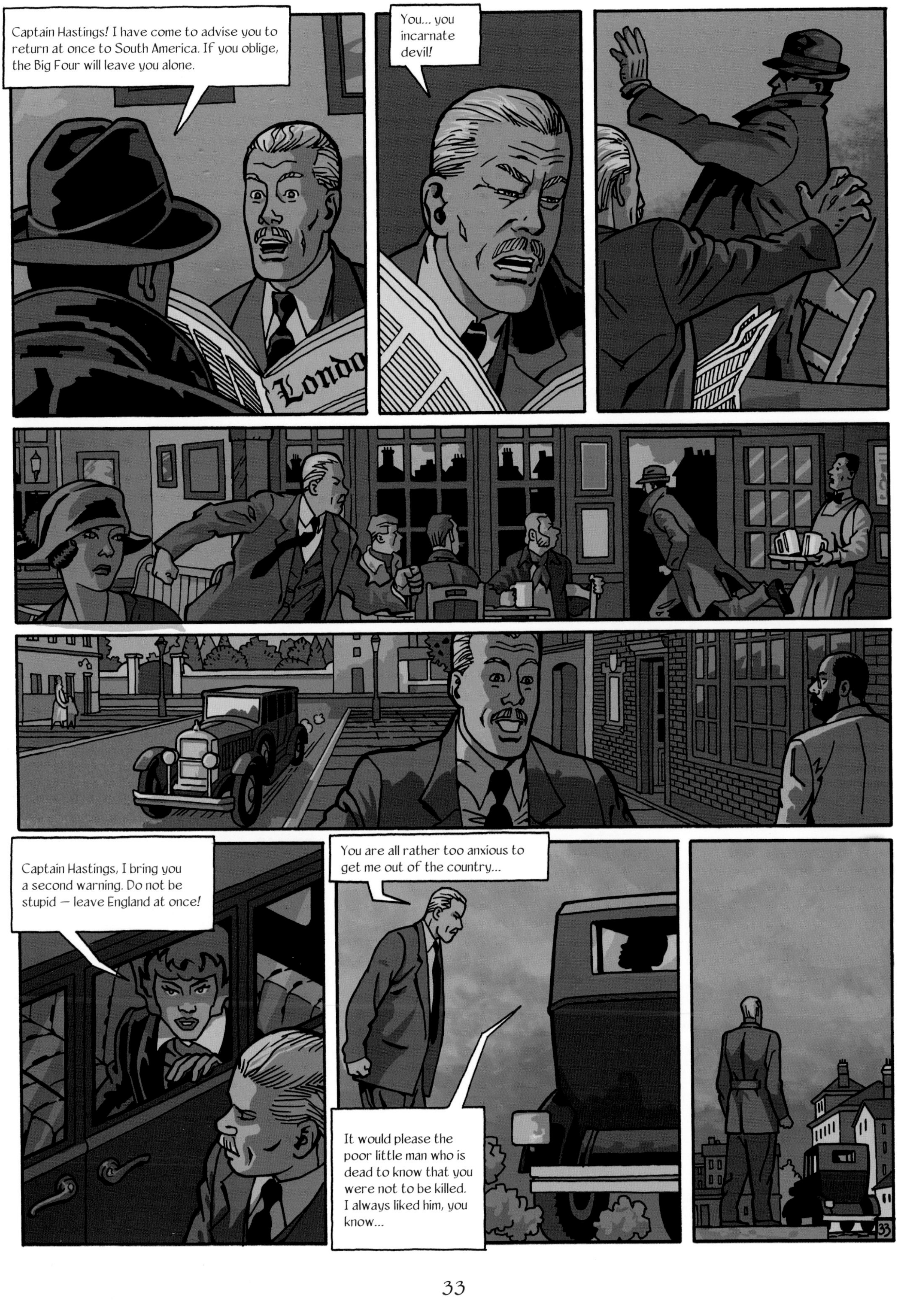
Captain Hastings! I have come to advise you to return at once to South America. If you oblige, the Big Four will leave you alone.
Londo
You... you incarnate devil!
Captain Hastings, I bring you a second warning. Do not be stupid — leave England at once!
You are all rather too anxious to get me out of the country...
It would please the poor little man who is dead to know that you were not to be killed. I always liked him, you know...

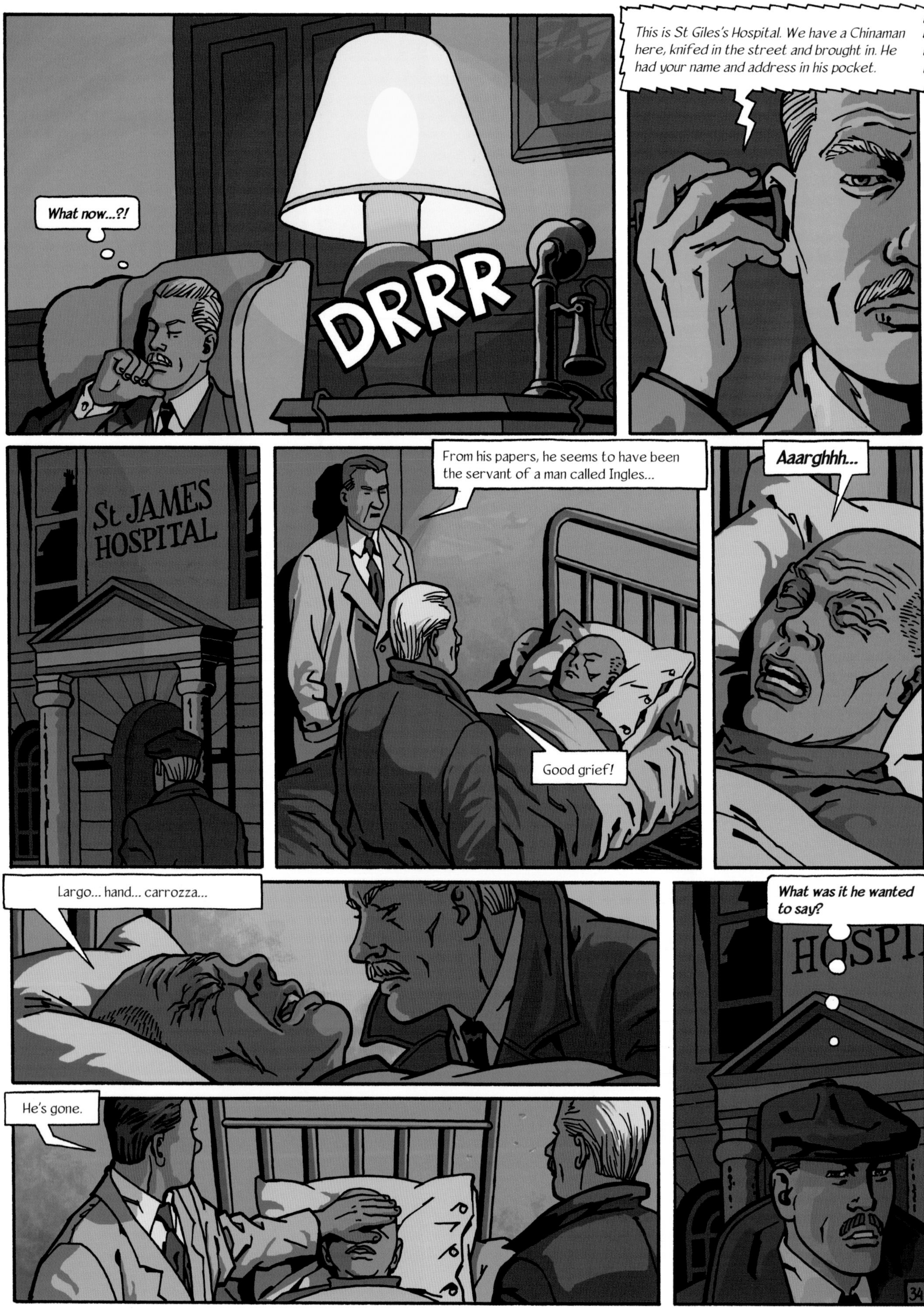
What now...?!
DRRR
This is St Giles's Hospital. We have a Chinaman here, knifed in the street and brought in. He had your name and address in his pocket.
St JAMES HOSPITAL
From his papers, he seems to have been the servant of a man called Ingles...
Good grief!
Aaarghhh...
Largo... hand... carrozza...
What was it he wanted to say?
HOSPI
He's gone.
34

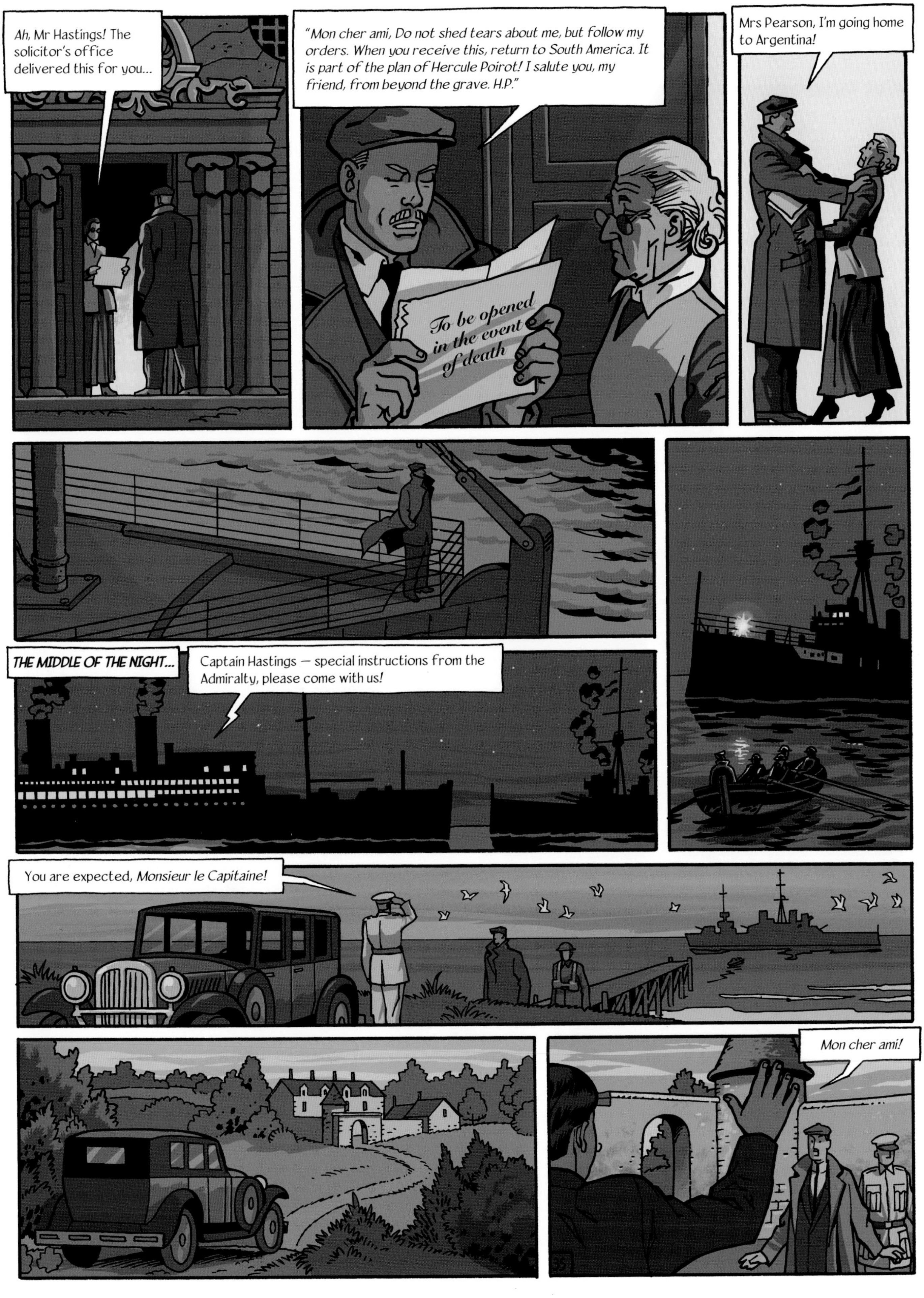
Ah, Mr Hastings! The solicitor's office delivered this for you...
"Mon cher ami, Do not shed tears about me, but follow my orders. When you receive this, return to South America. It is part of the plan of Hercule Poirot! I salute you, my friend, from beyond the grave. H.P."
To be opened in the event of death
Mrs Pearson, I'm going home to Argentina!
THE MIDDLE OF THE NIGHT...
Captain Hastings – special instructions from the Admiralty, please come with us!
You are expected, Monsieur le Capitaine!
Mon cher ami!

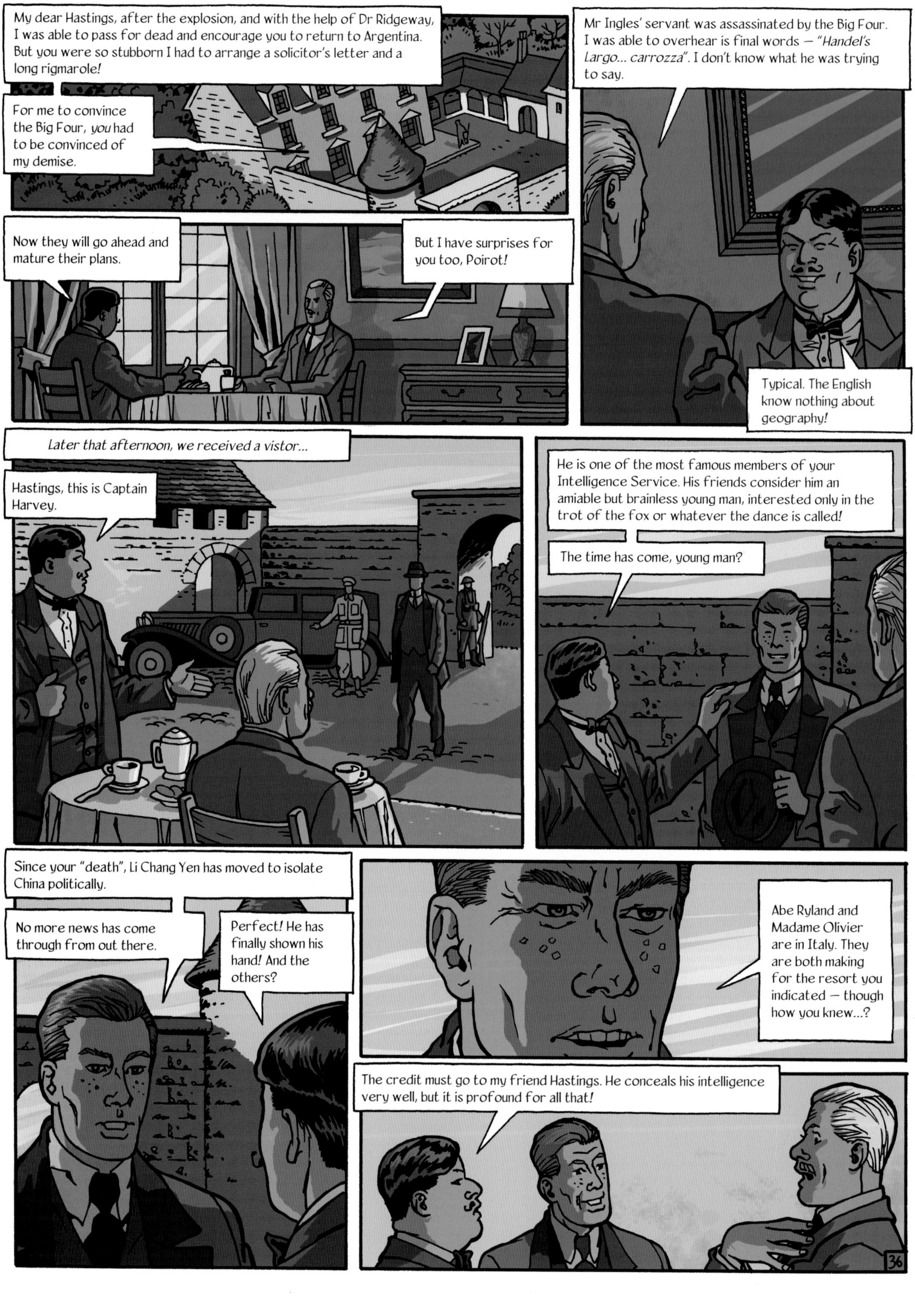

My dear Hastings, after the explosion, and with the help of Dr Ridgeway, I was able to pass for dead and encourage you to return to Argentina. But you were so stubborn I had to arrange a solicitor's letter and a long rigmarole!
For me to convince the Big Four, *you* had to be convinced of my demise.
Mr Ingles' servant was assassinated by the Big Four. I was able to overhear is final words — *"Handel's Largo... carrozza"*. I don't know what he was trying to say.
Now they will go ahead and mature their plans.
But I have surprises for you too, Poirot!
Typical. The English know nothing about geography!
Later that afternoon, we received a vistor...
Hastings, this is Captain Harvey.
He is one of the most famous members of your Intelligence Service. His friends consider him an amiable but brainless young man, interested only in the trot of the fox or whatever the dance is called!
The time has come, young man?
Since your "death", Li Chang Yen has moved to isolate China politically.
No more news has come through from out there.
Perfect! He has finally shown his hand! And the others?
Abe Ryland and Madame Olivier are in Italy. They are both making for the resort you indicated — though how you knew...?
The credit must go to my friend Hastings. He conceals his intelligence very well, but it is profound for all that!
36

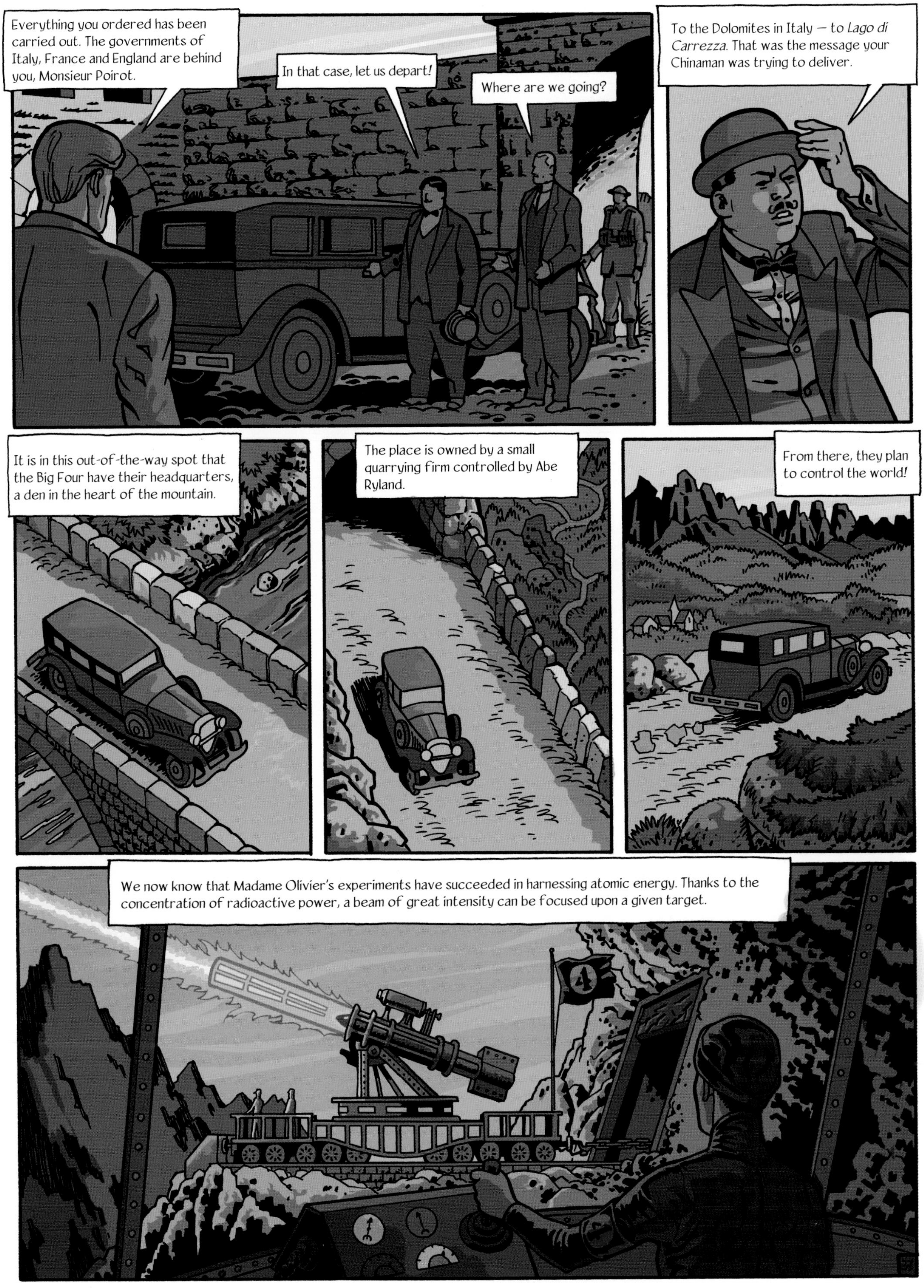
Everything you ordered has been carried out. The governments of Italy, France and England are behind you, Monsieur Poirot.
In that case, let us depart!
Where are we going?
To the Dolomites in Italy — to *Lago di Carrezza*. That was the message your Chinaman was trying to deliver.
It is in this out-of-the-way spot that the Big Four have their headquarters, a den in the heart of the mountain.
The place is owned by a small quarrying firm controlled by Abe Ryland.
From there, they plan to control the world!
We now know that Madame Olivier's experiments have succeeded in harnessing atomic energy. Thanks to the concentration of radioactive power, a beam of great intensity can be focused upon a given target.

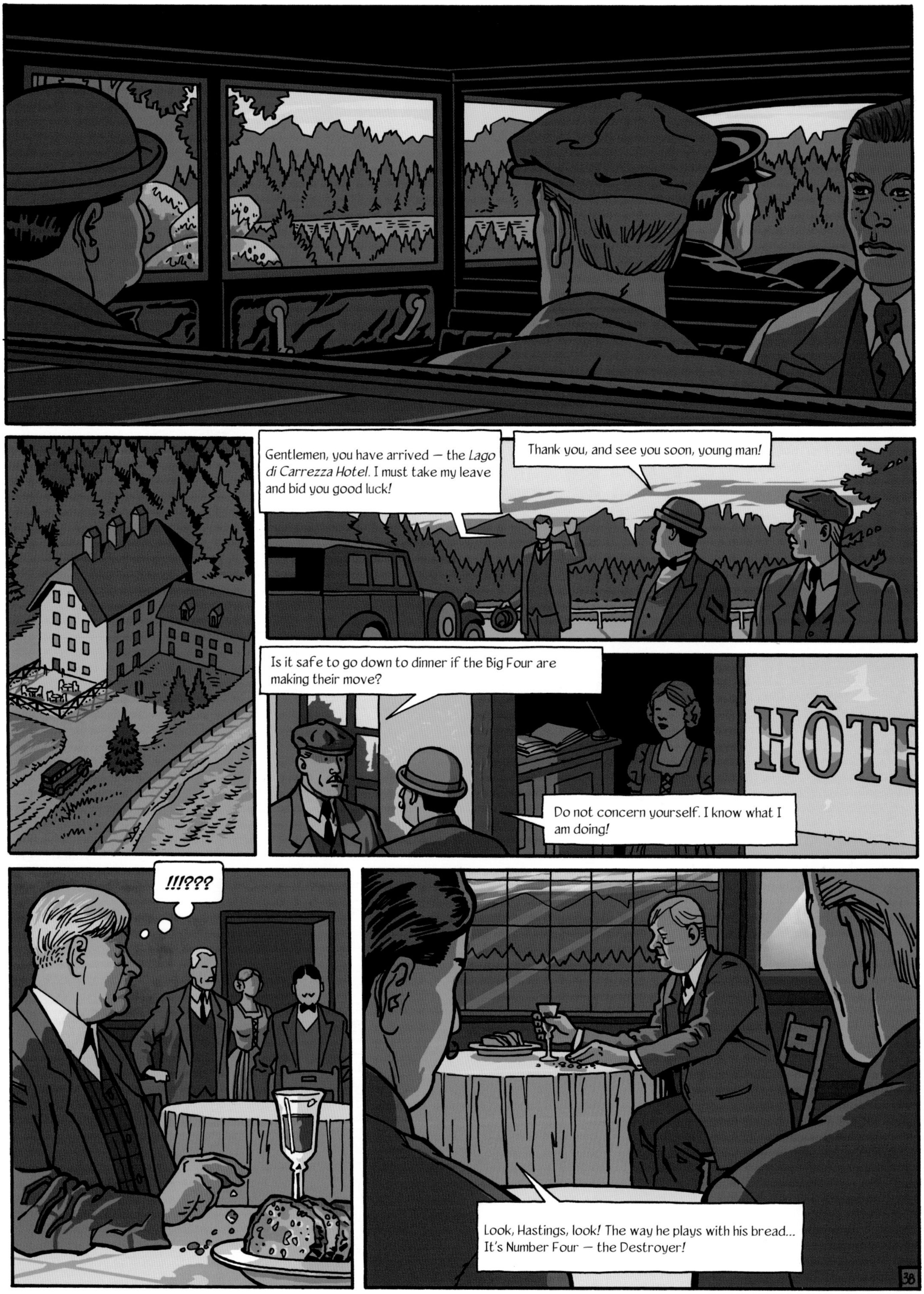
Gentlemen, you have arrived — the *Lago di Carrezza Hotel*. I must take my leave and bid you good luck!
Thank you, and see you soon, young man!
Is it safe to go down to dinner if the Big Four are making their move?
HÔTE
Do not concern yourself. I know what I am doing!
!!!???
Look, Hastings, look! The way he plays with his bread... It's Number Four — the Destroyer!
38

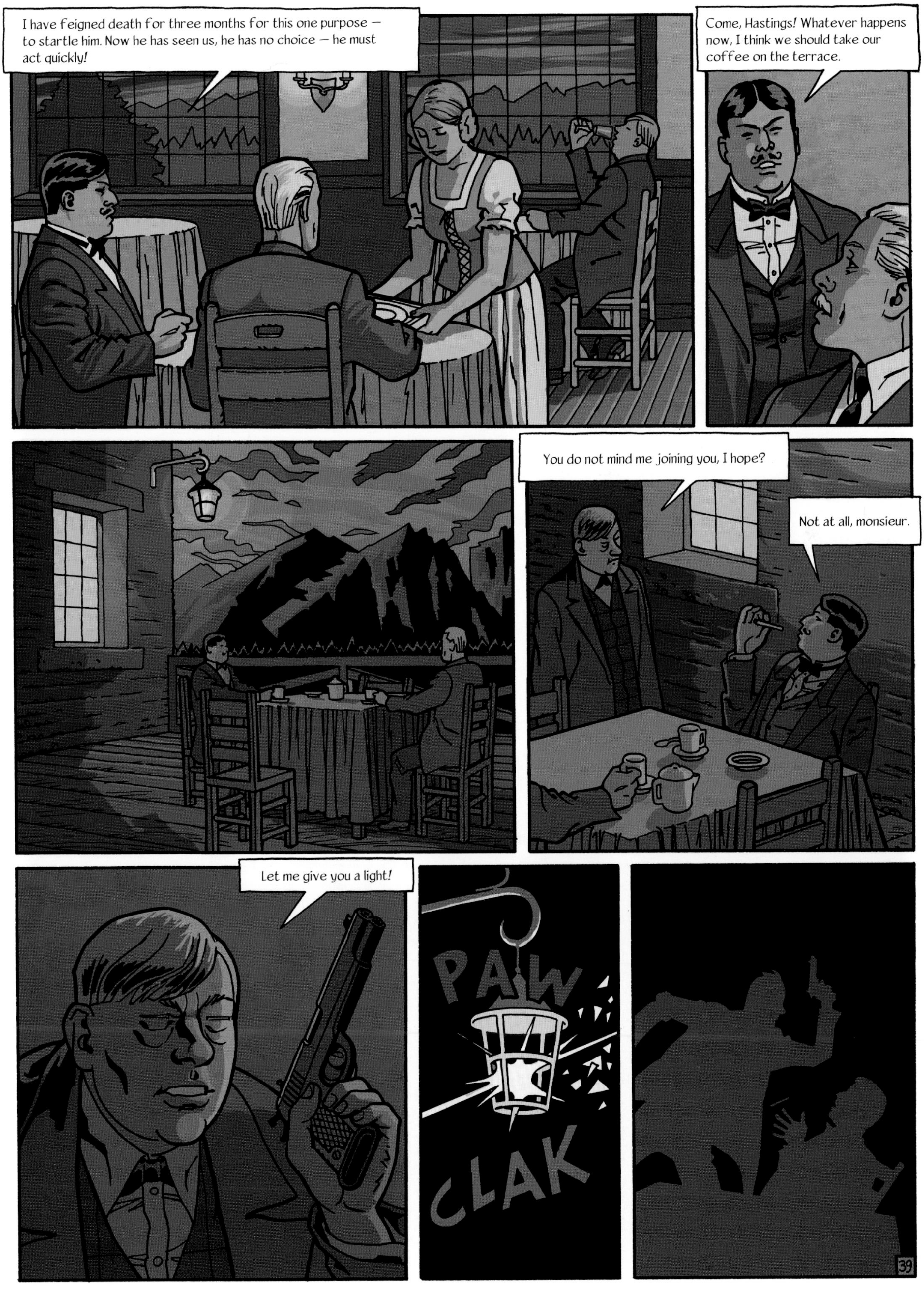
I have feigned death for three months for this one purpose — to startle him. Now he has seen us, he has no choice — he must act quickly!
Come, Hastings! Whatever happens now, I think we should take our coffee on the terrace.
You do not mind me joining you, I hope?
Not at all, monsieur.
Let me give you a light!
PAW
CLAK
39

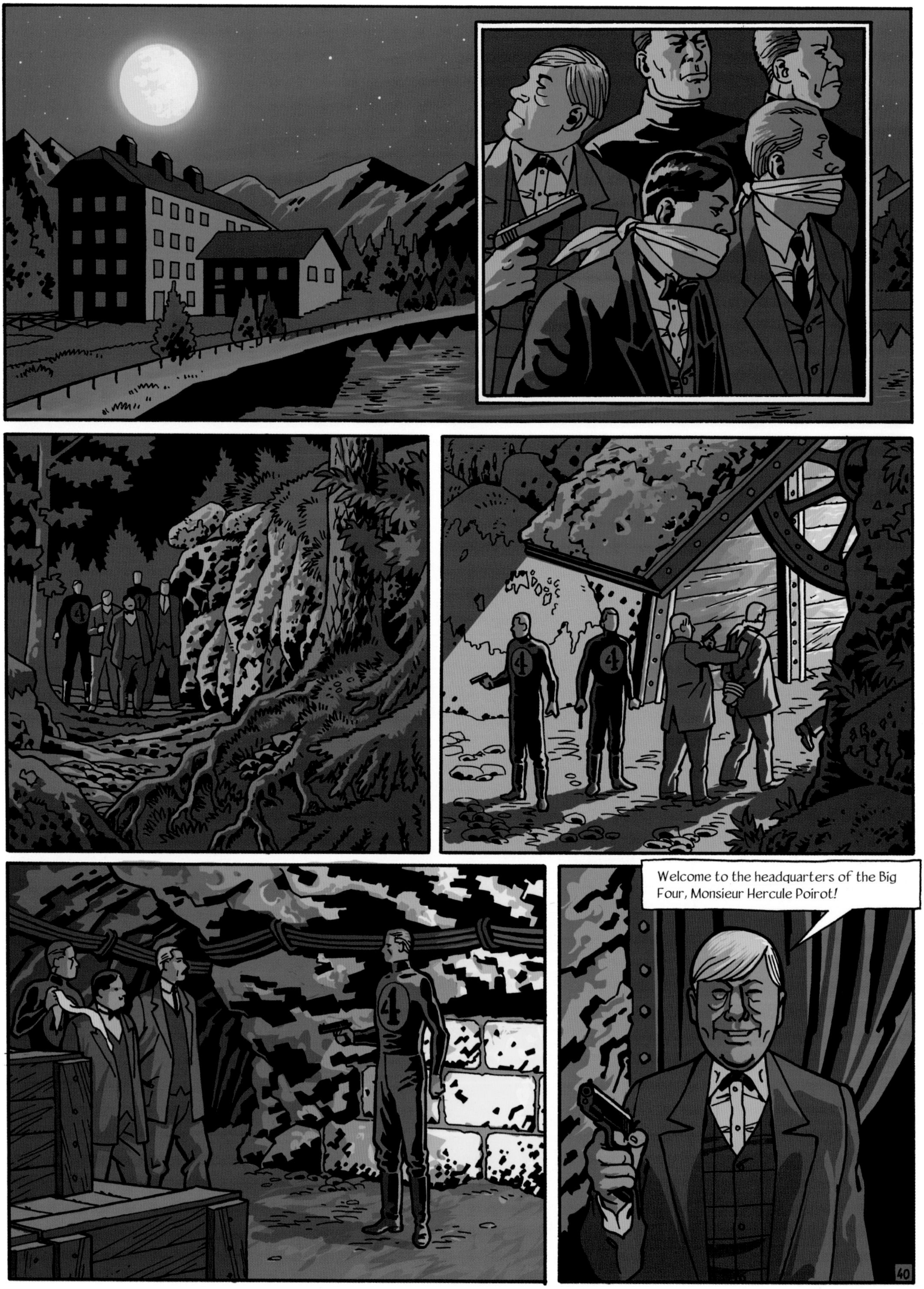
Welcome to the headquarters of the Big Four, Monsieur Hercule Poirot!
40

Come this way. Your arrival will be something of a surprise to my colleagues.

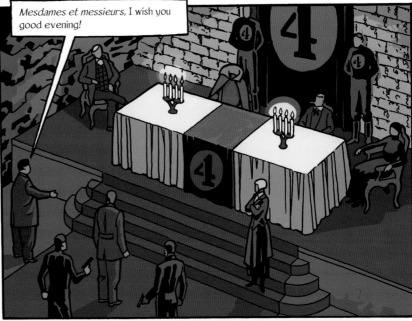

Mesdames et messieurs, I wish you good evening!

This man is not Hercule Poirot!

Then who is he?

I know! It's Achille Poirot — Hercule Poirot's twin brother!

Impossible!

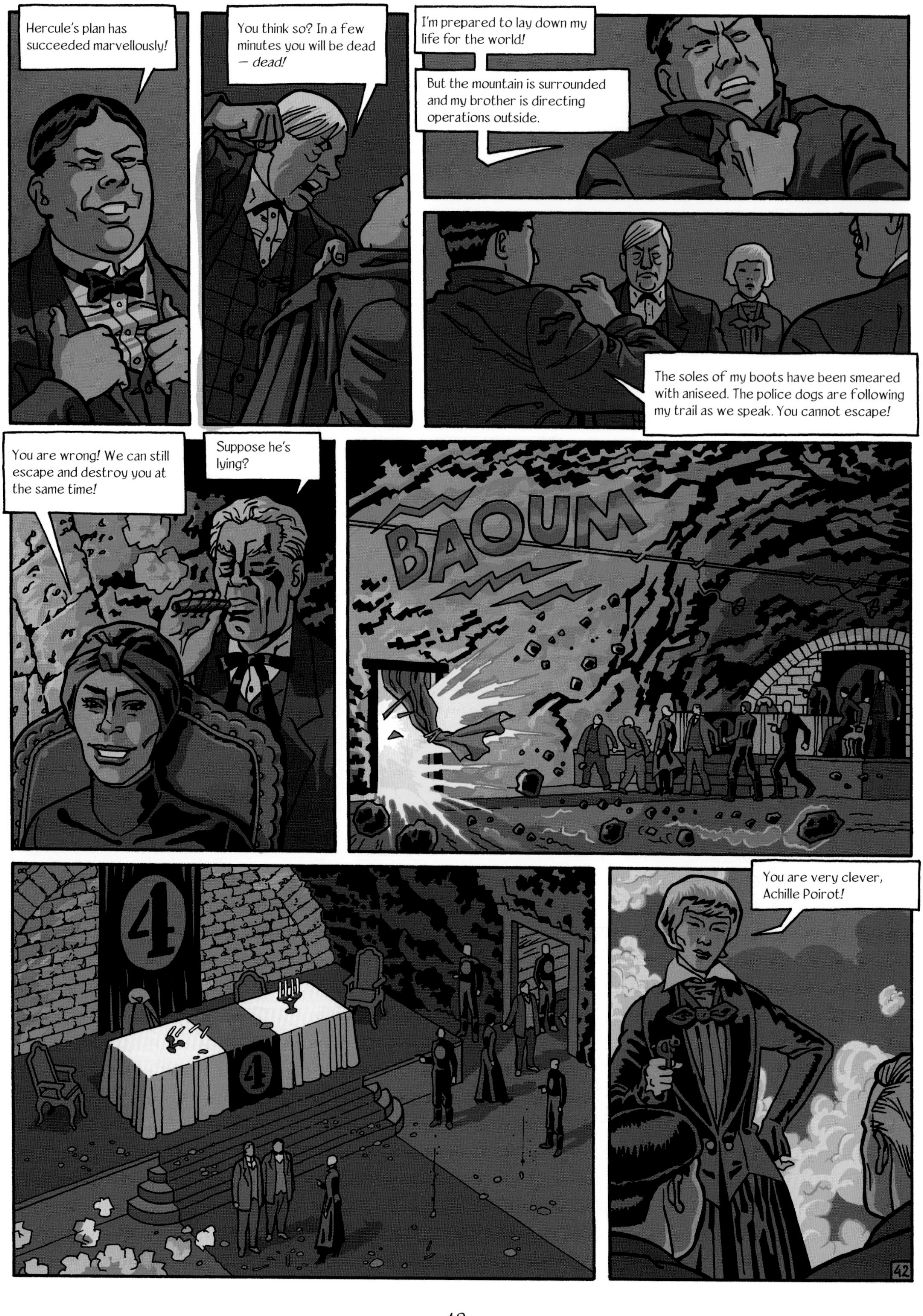

Hercule's plan has succeeded marvellously!
You think so? In a few minutes you will be dead — *dead!*
I'm prepared to lay down my life for the world!
But the mountain is surrounded and my brother is directing operations outside.
The soles of my boots have been smeared with aniseed. The police dogs are following my trail as we speak. You cannot escape!
You are wrong! We can still escape and destroy you at the same time!
Suppose he's lying?
BAOUM
4
4
You are very clever, Achille Poirot!
42

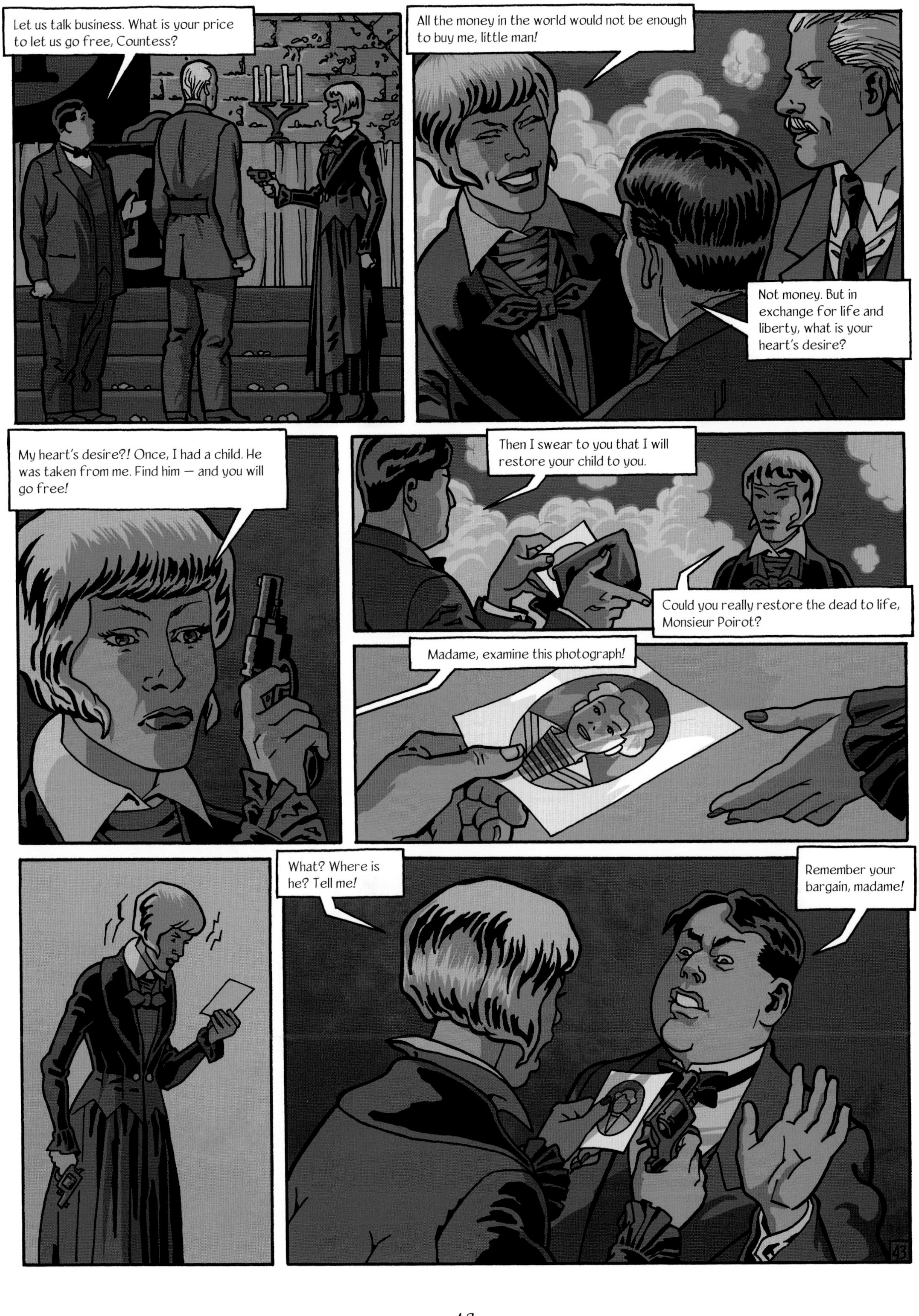
Let us talk business. What is your price to let us go free, Countess?
All the money in the world would not be enough to buy me, little man!
Not money. But in exchange for life and liberty, what is your heart's desire?
My heart's desire?! Once, I had a child. He was taken from me. Find him — and you will go free!
Then I swear to you that I will restore your child to you.
Could you really restore the dead to life, Monsieur Poirot?
Madame, examine this photograph!
What? Where is he? Tell me!
Remember your bargain, madame!
43

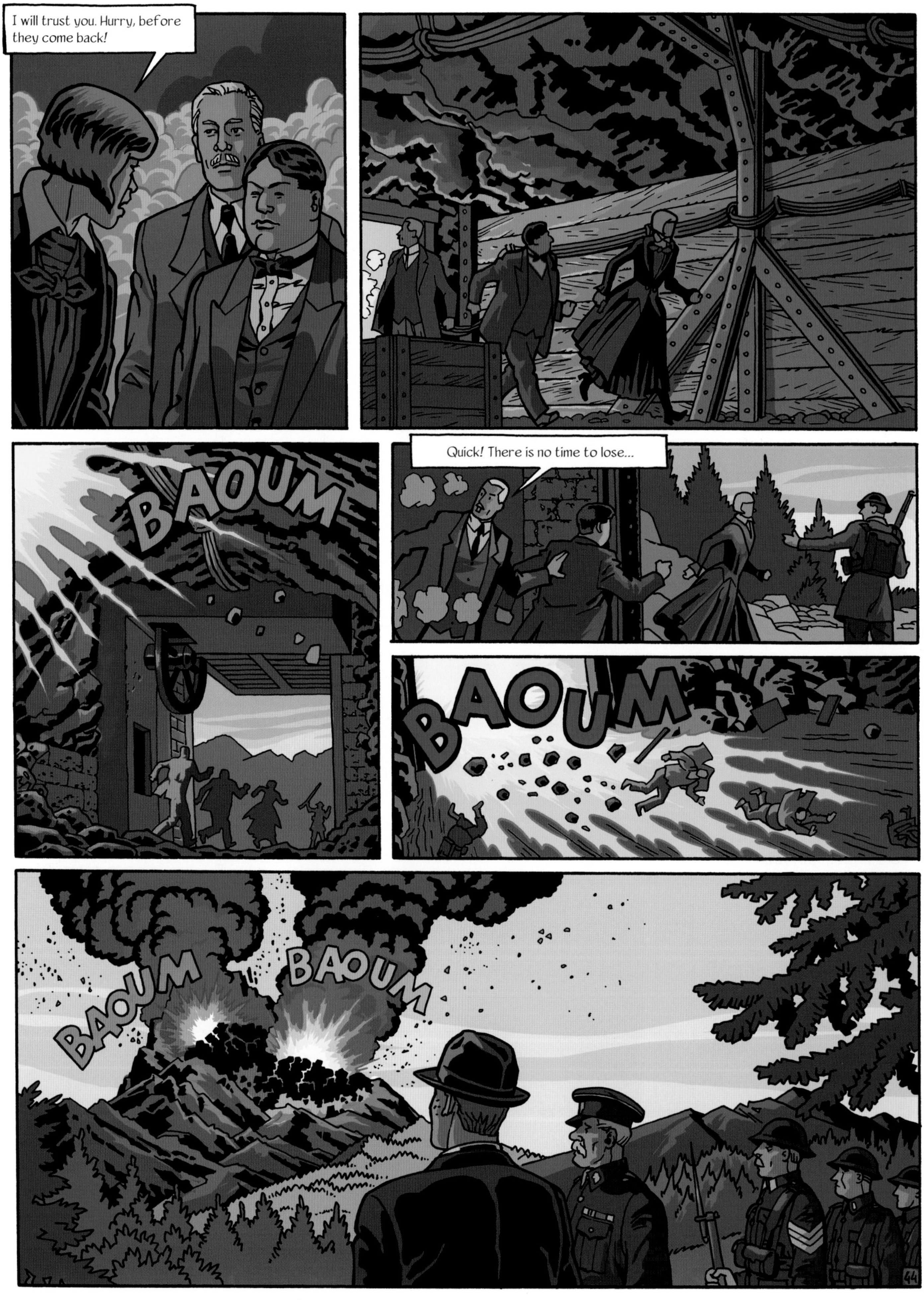

I will trust you. Hurry, before they come back!
BAOUM
Quick! There is no time to lose...
BAOUM
BAOUM
BAOUM
44

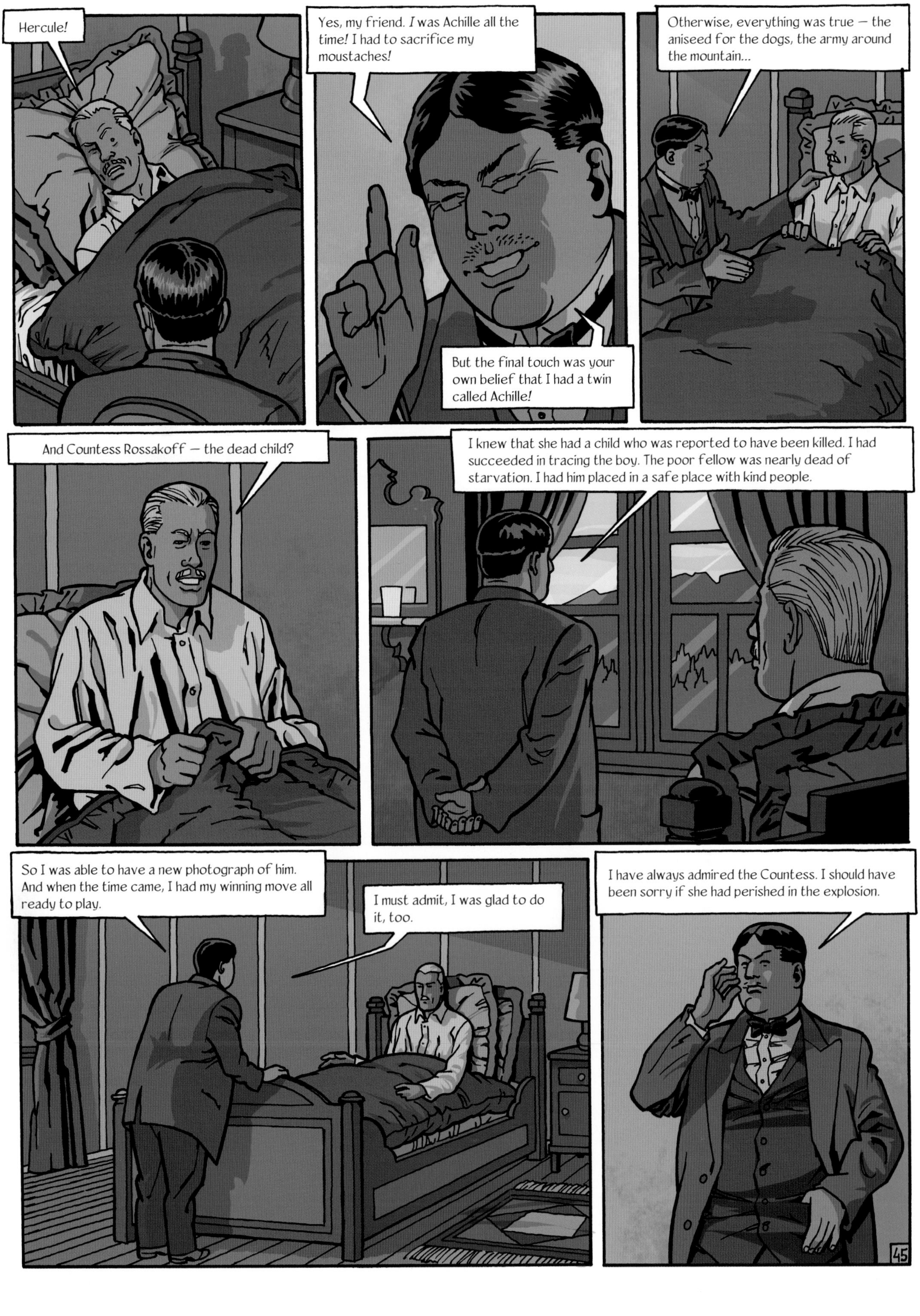

Hercule!
Yes, my friend. *I* was Achille all the time! I had to sacrifice my moustaches!
But the final touch was your own belief that I had a twin called Achille!
Otherwise, everything was true — the aniseed for the dogs, the army around the mountain...
And Countess Rossakoff — the dead child?
I knew that she had a child who was reported to have been killed. I had succeeded in tracing the boy. The poor fellow was nearly dead of starvation. I had him placed in a safe place with kind people.
So I was able to have a new photograph of him. And when the time came, I had my winning move all ready to play.
I must admit, I was glad to do it, too.
I have always admired the Countess. I should have been sorry if she had perished in the explosion.
45

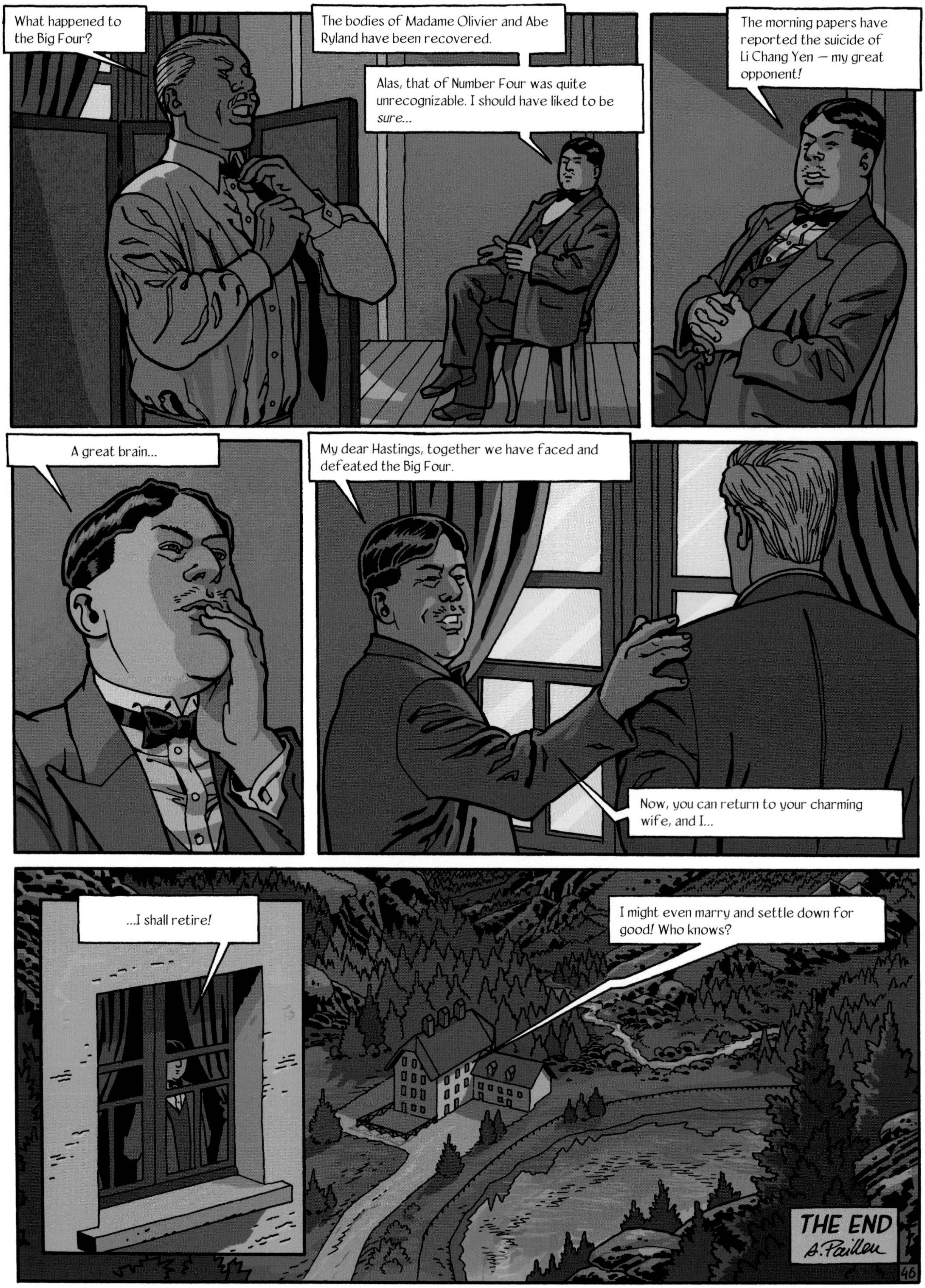
What happened to the Big Four?
The bodies of Madame Olivier and Abe Ryland have been recovered.
Alas, that of Number Four was quite unrecognizable. I should have liked to be *sure*...
The morning papers have reported the suicide of Li Chang Yen — my great opponent!
A great brain...
My dear Hastings, together we have faced and defeated the Big Four.
Now, you can return to your charming wife, and I...
...I shall retire!
I might even marry and settle down for good! Who knows?
THE END
A. Paillou
46